ROSE
THE AWAKENING

ROSE
THE AWAKENING

KRYS KINGSTON

Book Guild Publishing

First published in Great Britain in 2016 by
The Book Guild Ltd
9 Priory Business Park
Wistow Road, Kibworth
Leicestershire, LE8 0RX
Freephone: 0800 999 2982
www.bookguild.co.uk
Email: info@bookguild.co.uk
Twitter: @bookguild

Typeset in Adobe Garamond

Printed and bound in Great Britain by
CPI Group (UK) Ltd, Croydon, CR0 4YY

ISBN 978 1 910508 90 9

British Library Cataloguing in Publication Data.
A catalogue record for this book is available from the British Library.

To my sister for never objecting to my late night writing sessions when this book was first being drafted.

And to everyone who has contributed in some shape or form with early edits, plot suggestions, fact checks, sanity checks and moral support.

PROLOGUE

I lie on the forest floor, staring up at the twinkling sky above me. I can feel my heart beginning to slow and the rising of my chest becoming less frequent as I struggle with my last breath.

The pain is agonising and I need relief. Then it comes. Limb by limb, my body begins to numb. The darkness comes over me like a wave and I slip gracefully into the nothingness that is death.

We are all destined to die. That is our mortal fate. But what if death's clock could be altered? What if the ticking hands of time could be stopped? What price would you be willing to pay? What sacrifices would you be willing to make to obtain such a gift, such a curse?

And so my tale unfolds before you. Take heed, for this is not a tale of light and dark. This is a tale of shadows; the in-between forgotten spaces that lie between the borders of good and evil.

PART I

CHAPTER 1

To understand how it is that I came to part with my life at such an early age, I must take you back to the day I met Mr Oliver Weir.

It was a dull cool day in November. The year was 1887. I had just awoke and lay staring up at the damp stain on the ceiling above me. The images from my dream were still fresh in my mind, haunting me.

The dreams started coming to me after my father died six years ago. And now they were occurring more frequently.

They always began much the same…

I am running as fast as my legs can carry me, weaving through a dark forest. Clutched within my hand is a single red rose, I can feel the sting of its thorns piercing my flesh.

From beyond the darkness I can hear my father's voice calling me.

As I enter into a small clearing, my fear dissolves into wonder. Before me is a body of water glistening brightly in the moonlight. I am drawn forth. Kneeling I peer into the water at my reflection. I am altered. My dull and ill-managed hair is a mass of vibrant copper spirals. My skin is as smooth and pale as porcelain, and my eyes shine brilliant green like emeralds…

For years the images had been the same, the same dark forest, the same feeling of being chased, the same transformation. But lately they had begun to last longer, to reveal more. This time I could almost make out the reflection of a figure standing over me.

I rose from my bed and quickly tugged a brush through my tangled curls. I caught a glimpse of myself in my dressing mirror and let out a long deep sigh.

My father died when I was nine. He had made a good living and our life had been a comfortable one. For a time we managed to live off the dower Mother had received and led a normal life. Over time Mother had to let go most of the staff as she simply could not afford to keep them on and eventually, as her income dwindled to a pittance, Mother decided to sell Blythewood, our family home.

Now I barely recognised my reflection staring back at me. My skin was pale, but not a milky complection that one might admire. It was colourless. Transparent. The kind of pale that comes from poor nutrition and a lack of exposure to sunlight. My once vibrant locks had grown thin and dull and my garments had been mended and altered so many times that there was barely an unstitched square of fabric left on them.

To provide for us, Mother went into service as a housemaid and managed to let some rooms in London on what little earnings she had.

I pulled open the bedroom door. Mother was seated at the table across from a gentleman, her long slender body poised with concentrated perfection.

The gentleman stood to greet me as I approached.

'This must be the lovely Rose,' he said and pulled out an empty chair beside him while motioning for me to sit.

Hesitantly, I sat and poured myself a cup of tea. The room around me grew noticably colder.

'Rose, darling, this is Mr Weir.' My parents were the only ones ever to address me as Rose. Rose is my second name. My full name is Kirstin Rose Elizabeth.

'Please, call me Oliver.' As he spoke he gave a subtle crooked smile which forced small wrinkles to appear in the corners of each of his ebony-coloured eyes. Mr Weir was a handsome man. There was no doubt about that. He was tall and slender, and although his thick black hair was beginning to grey, he looked to be no more than in his mid-to-late thirties.

Mother explained that he had come to offer her employment. Apparently, a previous housemaid of ours, Prudence, had also been under the employ of Mr Weir and had spoken a great deal of Mother and of how she was now in service. He had only recently thought to inquire into the matter as his house had been fully staffed until a short while ago.

His eyes wandered over me. My cheeks grew warm and he smiled at the sight of this. I was suddenly embarrassed to have received such a gentleman in our simple home. The room in which we were seated served as kitchen, dining and sitting room. Off of it was a separate bedchamber with a single bed and small wardrobe and dressing table that the two of us shared – although most nights Mother fell asleep out here in her chair in front of the fire.

I suppose we were lucky to have as much as we did. Others nearby were not so fortunate; I had seen families with as many as eight living in one room all together.

Quietly I sipped my tea and listened to them continue their conversation. They discussed the terms of her service and what the position would entail. Why did he come to see to this matter personally? Surely he had a housekeeper who could have handled the arrangements.

Mr Weir stood, signalling their conversation had concluded. His tall slender figure towered over me, his shadow cloaking me in its cool darkness. I shivered.

As Mother fetched the gentleman's cloak and hat I attempted to stand to bid him farewell, only I found I could not rise; it was as if I were fixed to my very seat. How strange.

Taking note of my lack of propriety, Mr Weir's sharp black eyes fixed on mine as he took a step towards me. I inhaled sharply.

Leaning forward, he took my hand in his and lingered for a moment before he pressed it against his lips.

5

'Good day, Rose,' he uttered as he stepped out into the small alleyway. The clicking of his heels echoed through the fog as they met the uneven cobbles beneath him, getting gradually fainter as he departed.

Closing the door, Mother quickly turned towards me. 'What has got into you, Kirstin? You were as quiet as a church mouse. And since when do we not rise when a guest takes his leave?'

Repentantly I lowered my head. How could I explain my behaviour if I did not fully understand it myself? Never before had I felt such uneasiness towards another.

'Kirstin, you are not a child anymore. You really must learn to behave like a lady.'

'Yes, Mother. Forgive me.'

'Let us not dwell on it further. Go and get changed into something warmer. I need to go to the market and I want you to come with me.'

In the bedroom the air filled with dust as I jerked open the wardrobe doors. There was little to choose from. I had long ago outgrown the dresses from my childhood and now relied on hand-me-downs from Mother's employers.

The garments were all simple so I could easily dress myself. Gone were the days of lady's maids and corsets. These were luxuries that we could no longer afford.

I took off the threadbare clothes I had on and randomly pulled out several petticoats and a dress of slightly thicker material. This would have to do.

It was a miserable day and as we approached the market the air became thick with the stifling stench of rotting meat. Mother grasped my hand and led me quickly past the ghastly sight of butchered animals. The putrid smell of blood was becoming stronger with each step.

Voices swirled around me shouting cost and weight. Butchered cows swayed back and forth off their filthy rusted hooks. The people around me became a blur, ravenous carnivores wading through pools of blood. I could usually just shake off my disgust, but today my stomach was exceptionally weak and my head grew dizzy.

Pushing my way through the herd of people I caught up with Mother. She pulled out a piece of paper from her pocket and instructed the butcher as to her cut of meat. Normally, we simply took the offcuts, whatever morsel we could afford that week. But as the butcher's sharpened cleaver hacked away at the belly of the swine before him, I knew that today we were getting prime meat. But why, how could she possibly afford it?

I was thankful when we started home, but the stench of the market seemed to follow us. Passers-by disappeared into the thick fog and re-emerged in the form of slaughtered cows and headless chickens. I could taste the splattered blood fresh upon my lips.

Our journey home seemed endless. Mother spoke sporadically but to me her words seemed like faint mumbles. We entered into a meaningless conversation washed away by the grotesque visions and thoughts that haunted me.

Eventually we arrived home, and for once I was glad to be there.

I had just begun helping Mother put the provisions away when she handed me a letter. I was instructed to leave immediately and deliver it by hand and wait for a reply. I looked at the address. It was in Holborn, which was a fair distance on foot. I wondered whom it was for.

Holding my breath, I stepped back into the pungent odour of the streets.

CHAPTER 2

The streets of London were dense with people. As I weaved through the crowds my mind began to wander back to my earlier encounter with Mr Weir. I could still feel the sensation of his rough lips against my hand. The invasion of his eyes into my very soul.

After Father died everything changed.

His death had cast a dark shadow over our lives from which we could not escape.

Since then, my exposure to the world of gentle society had grown very limited. It was a different breed that dwelled in the East End, but for the most part at least you knew where you stood with people.

Meeting Mr Weir seemed to awaken something within me. It was as if a part of me that had lain dormant had awoken.

My feet were aching by the time I finally reached my destination. The houses in this area were all very much alike, tall but modest. I retrieved the address from my pocket and continued until I reached the specified house number. Tapping lightly upon the solid red door, I waited for someone to answer.

Moments later I could hear footsteps approaching and the door was opened. At the threshold stood a short portly man with grey hair. He looked down at me quizzically.

'Yes. Who are you?' he asked.

'Good morning, Sir, I have a letter for you,' I said, handing him the letter.

His short stubby fingers fumbled to open the envelope. He lifted a pair of spectacles to his eyes and read its contents with astute concentration.

'Wait here a moment, please,' he told me before stepping inside for a moment and returning with a brown paper package. 'Take this to Mr Weir, at this address.' He handed me the parcel and a piece of paper with Mr Weir's address scribbled on it.

'Thank you. Good day to you,' I managed to say before the door slammed in my face. How peculiar indeed.

I meandered through the streets rather slowly, dreading my next destination. My feet were sorer than ever and my fingers felt frozen from the bitter-cold air that nipped at their exposed tips.

I arrived shortly at Mr Weir's. I passed through the creaking wrought-iron gate and continued down the tiled pathway. I noticed that the tiles needed a good scrubbing; I wondered how long he had gone without adequate help.

Mr Weir's house was a row house of no particular dissimilarity to those around it. It was of common size for its location and there was nothing grandiose about it. However, it was large enough to require more than a couple of servants to care for it. Mother would certainly have her work cut out for her here.

I approached the front door and, as I was too short to reach the brass lion's head that served as a knocker, I instead rapped my frozen hand loudly against the hard glossy black surface.

After a few moments of waiting, the door was answered. Before me stood a man of average height and weight. He looked middle-aged and he wore a freshly pressed black suit and white shirt; this must be Mr Weir's butler.

'Good afternoon, Sir, I have a parcel for Mr Weir,' I explained.

'You must be Mrs Maines' daughter. The Master has been expecting you. Come inside.' Leading me inside, he placed my cloak and bonnet on a stand and escorted me down a long narrow hallway. The house was dark and cold. The narrow walls seemed to close around me and it was not until we had finally reached the end and stepped into the drawing room that I could once again breathe easily.

I turned to thank Mr Weir's butler, but he had already disappeared from view. As I fully entered the room Mr Weir tucked a letter he had been reading into his pocket and stood to greet me.

'Ah, Rose, I am so fortunate to have the pleasure of your company twice in one day. Please sit down.' He motioned with his hand towards an empty chair.

I did not sit down. I stepped forward and handed him the parcel. When it was safely in his hands I took one step backwards. Mr Weir's lean spidery fingers unwrapped the brown paper. The fire crackled beside him giving off a warm glow. His long slender shadow danced across the green walls.

The room was similar to Father's old drawing room. The shelves were filled with books and I noticed a small photograph on one of them. I recognised Mr Weir and with him in the picture was a woman and child. It reminded me of a similar family portrait we had had taken when Father had been alive.

'I must insist you sit down, Rose. You see, as long as you are standing, proper etiquette demands that I must also stand and I would much rather be seated.'

I did as he requested and once Mr Weir had sat down again he placed his parcel down on the floor beside his chair. Curious, I looked inside: the box contained a book but I could not clearly make out the title.

After a moment of silence Mr Weir spoke. 'Thank you for delivering my parcel, Rose. I trust you had no difficulty finding the place?'

'I encountered no difficulty whatsoever, Sir. Would you be so kind to call me Kirstin, or Kirstin Rose, if you must?' I asked as politely as I could manage.

The side of Mr Weir's mouth curled up into a smile. 'Your father called you Rose, did he not?'

'Yes, Sir, he did.' I was surprised and unsure of how he came to know this information.

The warm gentle glow of the fire illuminated Mr Weir's face, casting hollow dark circles around his eyes. 'How did he die?'

'Pneumonia. At least that is what the doctor said.'

'And you doubted his diagnosis?'

'I have little experience with death, Mr Weir, so cannot claim to know what causes it. It is just… just that it seemed so strange to me that someone could catch their death so easily from a bit of poor weather.'

My mind wandered back to the day my father became ill. He had been returning to London from some business that had called him away, as it often did. The weather had been particularly harsh that week, and although it was perhaps ill advised, Father refused to wait to make his journey home.

En route, the carriage became stuck in the mud and could not be freed. Each attempt he and his driver made to free the wheels only caused them to sink deeper. Eventually, they had no choice but to continue on foot.

That evening I had stayed by the window waiting for him to return. As the night drew on and my eyes grew tired I could feel my body becoming heavy – slipping away into that state between sleep and awake. As my eyes flicked open and closed, I saw a slender shadow, a faint figure approaching the gate; it was my father.

His body was hunched over beneath the weight of the heavy downpour as he staggered towards the house. He collapsed before even reaching the threshold; those had been the last steps he ever took.

My gaze was locked on the ring my father had given me on his deathbed. The ruby stone shimmered in the firelight. I recalled his gaunt face staring up at me, whispering my name through shallow breaths.

'Rose…'

'Sorry did you say something?'

'I asked how it was he became ill. What was the cause of it? But if it troubles you too much, we can speak of something else.'

'Yes, I mean I do not like to think on it.'

'Very well. Do you read?'

'Pardon?'

'Do you read? I noticed you admiring my collection of books when you entered.'

'I can read, yes.'

'There is the ability to read and then there is the desire to do so – do you enjoy reading for pleasure?'

My eyes glanced back towards the shelves of books and fixed upon the photograph once more. 'That photograph – is that your family?'

His body grew stiff and the room suddenly felt cooler. 'That is my wife, Isabel, and our daughter, Anna.'

I had been under the misassumption that he was a bachelor. Perhaps his family lived in a country house somewhere and he simply came to London for business.

Mr Weir gazed into the blazing fire. Outside a light drizzle had begun to fall and in the distance I could hear soft rolls of thunder. 'My wife did not appreciate the amount of travel my occupation required. She did not understand the responsibilities I had…' He paused and I could tell it was difficult for him to speak. 'I came home one day and they were gone.'

'I'm so sorry,' I looked away – embarrassed to have brought it up. 'I had not realised. Forgive me.'

'How could you – how could you know?' His posture had once again softened. For a moment I felt pity for him and he could feel it. He lifted his eyes to mine. The glow of the fire was reflected within the two black spheres.

He rose from his seat and walked over to one of the shelves of books. Extending his hand he ran his index finger along the variously coloured spines, stopping seemingly at random and tipping forward his selection into his open hand.

'Here, I think you will enjoy this one,' he said, placing his copy of Charlotte Brontë's *Jane Eyre* in my lap.

'Thank you! I shan't keep you any longer. I really must be off.' I rose to leave and gave a slight bow to my host.

'Please take my carriage. A lady should not walk such far distances if it can be helped otherwise.'

'That is very kind of you to offer, but I prefer to go by foot.' Why had I refused? My feet ached at the very thought of my long journey home.

Mr Weir did not insist and I was grateful for it. He saw me out and once on my way home I felt relieved to be free of his company.

CHAPTER 3

A strong gust of wind blew through the streets of London, causing the lamplight to flicker against the backdrop of the darkening indigo sky. I pulled my cloak tight around me and folded my arms close around my chest. The hard edges of the book pressed into me, but I made sure to keep it close.

Stepping into an adjacent alleyway, I sought shelter from the approaching storm. Its tall brick walls provided momentary protection against the cold wind.

There was a moment of silence – a pause, and then the sky opened up above me. The rain poured down relentlessly. Thunder rolled through the night air.

Someone followed, his footsteps growing louder behind me. Turning, I could not recognise the shadowy figure in the distance. Quickening my pace I hurried on. But the footsteps began to quicken as well, and as I turned down the next street so did my shadowy pursuer. I was most certainly being followed. But by whom?

My brisk walk had now become a run. The heavy drops of rain struck my face and obstructed my vision. I dashed through the darkened side streets, past empty doorways.

My chest was becoming heavy. My throat dry. The screams I tried to project lodged in my throat. Terrified, I willed my body to propel my legs faster, but they would not obey.

At last I fell and the ground rushed up towards me as I hit the cobbles. The book I had been holding so tightly was abandoned to an adjacent puddle. I heard the echoing clicks of footsteps approaching, I tried to stand, but it was no use. My legs had given way.

As the steps emerged out of the shadows, I closed my eyes tight and began to silently weep while I awaited my fate.

'It is all right, my dear – I do not intend to harm you!'

Opening my eyes, I saw Mr Weir standing over me. With a look of concern upon his face he held the dripping copy of *Jane Eyre* out towards me.

'Why are you following me?' I asked, my voice raised over the increasingly load claps of thunder. I was not sure if I was relived to see him.

'It was getting dark and I did not feel you should be walking alone. I am deeply sorry I frightened you. It is just that you had a bit of a head start on me and I was trying to catch up.' He extended his hand in order to help me up.

I accepted his gesture and slowly stood. Mr Weir gently placed his cloak around my shoulders. My legs were still a bit unstable but I could manage to walk with a bit of help. Offering his arm for extra support, he continued to escort me home.

The rain was weakening and the loud claps of thunder had calmed once again into a gentle grumbling roll. People emerged from their sheltered hiding places into the streets once more.

Mr Weir walked silently beside me. His mind always seemed to be somewhere else away from here.

We had now turned the corner on to my street. Turning to bid him farewell, I found that he no longer stood beside me.

Once inside I began to search for a lamp or candle to light. It was then that I noticed that the usual darkness was penetrated by a thin triangular beam of light stretching across the floor from behind the slightly ajar bedroom door. Placing Mr Weir's wet cloak on a chair, I walked towards the bedroom. The muffled sound of crying broke through the silence as I grew near.

Opening the door, I saw Mother leaning over the edge of the bed, her back quickly rising and falling as she choked back her tears. I entered the room and walked slowly towards her.

'Mother. What's wrong? Why are you crying?' Placing my hand upon her shoulder I tried to soothe her.

She slowly lifted her head and wiped away the falling tears. 'I am so sorry, Kirstin; I did not wish you to see me in such a state.' Her tears erupted once more. 'It…it is only that I have failed you. You deserve so much more. I should have sent you away to your uncle's after your father passed. Surely they could have provided better for you.'

'Hush, Mother, stop this. You are upsetting yourself. What has brought this on?' I asked.

'Seeing you today – the way you behaved. I have only myself to blame for your lack of propriety.'

I kneeled down before her and took her hands in mine. 'I would rather be unfortunate and ill mannered than to have lost both Mother and Father. Luckily, Father saw to it that I had a lady's upbringing and no matter what our circumstances that cannot be changed.'

'I suppose, but sometimes I do feel that it would have been better if I had been the one taken and not he.' She rose from the bed, wiping the tears away from her face with the sleeve of her blouse.

What had made her suddenly so melancholy?

Mother headed towards the door, but before exiting the room she turned to me. 'I love you, Kirstin, I love you very much.' With those words she continued out of the room, leaving me alone amongst the silent shadows.

I changed into my nightshift then quickly brushed out my damp and tangled hair. Kneeling beside my bed, I said my prayers and extinguished the candle.

As I slipped into my bed and pulled the covers up over me, my mind began to drift off, surrendering to the stream of familiar images.

The dream began the same way as all the others – the same dark woods, the same whispering voices coaxing me forward towards the glistening body of water.

As I approached the water and gazed into it, I saw that my reflection was that of my father and not my own. His voice was calm and soothing – barely more than a whisper – and he told me that everything would be all right, that all I need do was join him.

My hand closed tight around the crimson rose. A droplet of blood trickled down it then fell into the water, causing a circular wave of ripples that distorted my father's face. When the water stilled, I was staring down at the face of Mr Weir.

It was now Mr Weir's voice luring me to join him. Taunting me as he whispered my special name… 'ROSE!' I began to weep and as I did so his face vanished and I was left gazing at my own weary reflection.

CHAPTER 4

The next morning I awoke feeling unsettled.

Mother had made us a simple breakfast and was sitting at the table drinking a cup of tea when I emerged from my room. I poured myself a cup and sat down across from her.

She gazed at me for quite some time as if she were trying to read me. Breaking the silence she told me that we would be spending the day at Mr Weir's house while she went through her duties with the other staff.

To our surprise a carriage was waiting for us outside our home. Mr Weir must have sent it. I felt relieved – my feet ached and I had not been looking forward to taking the long journey again by foot – and then blushed at feeling grateful for his gesture.

The day was cool but quite dry, and the clouds were thick and dark. The carriage wobbled roughly along the uneven streets of the East End, towards our destination. There was enough room for four inside and Mother and I sat opposite each other. Mother's attention was fixed upon the world outside, whereas my gaze was upon her.

She had a soft gentle way about her, a delicacy that bordered on meekness. Her pale slender fingers were cupped in such a way as to support her angular jaw.

When the carriage finally came to a halt outside Mr Weir's house I watched as Mother was escorted inside. I was instructed to wait but, finding the carriage oppressive, chose to wait on the pavement.

As my eyes wandered over the brick facade of the house, some movement caught my attention – it was a curtain fluttering behind one of the second-storey windows.

Moments later Mr Weir emerged and slithered down the black-and-white tiled path to greet me. His long slender figure was dressed in black from head to toe.

His cold hard eyes met mine. I felt the heavy weight of his presence upon me. 'Come. I'm taking you to be fitted for some clothing more suitable for a young lady,' he said, aiding me back into the stifling black box of the carriage. Once we were both inside he snapped his fingers and the carriage began to move.

From my window, I watched as we passed the crowds of people. I recalled the outings Father and I used to take and for a moment I felt quite content. However, when I recalled whose company I shared my delight with it faded. Mr Weir, on the other hand, smiled in such a way at me that I could tell our time shared together meant a great deal to him.

A woman caught my attention as she went to work scrubbing the steps of one of the houses we passed. My thoughts turned to Mother. It made me very distraught to think of her working so hard for such an undeserving man. But why must I think so poorly of him? Had he not, thus far, shown me the greatest kindness?

My thoughts were interrupted by our carriage abruptly coming to a halt. Stepping out first, Mr Weir offered me his hand to assist me, which I accepted. Following him into the dressmaker's shop I waited on a small settee as he spoke to one of the women.

When they were ready for me, Mr Weir beckoned me over. I was aided on to a small wooden stool, following which the dressmaker took my measurements and jotted them down in a small black notebook.

On the spine of the book were the golden embossed initials 'O. W.' I recalled taking notice of other such books upon entering, which were alphabetically categorised on a shelf. Concluding that they were personalised for each regular customer, I knew that the initials stood for Mr Oliver Weir.

After my measurements had been taken I was assisted down and asked to sit back on the small settee and wait. The woman presented Mr Weir with an assortment of taffeta, faille, moiré, silk poplin, silk brocades and damask of different colours. She also showed him some popular patterns and explained which ones worked best with which fabrics.

Impatiently, I wound my finger around one of my long wayward curls. I had a feeling growing deep within my stomach that this charade was no more than some scheme to win my affection. The custom services of a dressmaker were something not many could afford, especially when so many ready-made styles were now available.

My stomach began to turn. To try and suppress the feeling I closed my eyes and rested my head in my hands. When I opened them, I saw Mr Weir advancing towards me with several different fabrics he had selected.

'What do you think of these, Rose?' I was still feeling very ill and the closeness of his presence was making it worse.

With what little enthusiasm I could manage, I agreed to what ever he thought was best. I could see he was becoming quite irritated with me. Frustrated, he threw the fabric back at the dressmaker and ordered her to have them ready as soon as possible.

Grabbing me by the hand he dragged me forcefully from the shop. Quickly giving his orders to the driver he shoved me inside the carriage and sat down close beside me.

As we drove on, he stared out of the window. When I could almost no longer bear the silence, he turned and addressed me. 'I am only trying to show you kindness, to provide you some release from your unfortunate circumstances, and yet you treat me as though I am not worth your acknowledgement. As if I were beneath you!'

'Please, Sir you scare me. The way you look upon me now – I fear for myself… I know not what to make of you.'

'I did not mean…' He reached his hand out towards me but I backed away.

'You stir feelings in me I find most confusing… You are a

stranger to me and yet you speak as though we have known each other for years.'

He leaned back, his posture relaxing a little. 'I am deeply sorry if I have behaved improperly or too familiarly, Rose. It is only that I do feel as though I have known you for years. Prudence, whom I understand worked in your house for quite some time, spoke of you constantly.'

'Of course – my mind is confused. Forgive me.' Perhaps he was speaking the truth. After all, what did I know of men and their behaviour? Turning away from him I watched as blurred silhouettes scurried towards unknown destinations, criss-crossing the crowded streets of London.

As we passed St James's Park I realised we were heading back to the Weir residence. Had I upset him so much that he could not bear to continue our excursion any further?

Once at our destination I hurried towards the house, Mr Weir followed close behind me.

The inside was just as dark and gloomy as before and I wondered if a single beam of light had ever danced across the walls of this old house. As I turned to Mr Weir, our eyes locked, the coldness of his burning into the warmth of mine. Shivering off the cold, I was suddenly light-headed and felt the darkness envelop me.

When I opened my eyes I realised I was on the floor. Had I fainted?

The butler was kneeling beside me.

'Are you all right, Miss?'

Sideways I watched as Mr Weir disappeared down the hallway into one of the rooms. 'Forgive me, I must have lost my footing.' I said, embarrassed and confused.

After helping me up, the butler led me towards the stairs and suggested I lie down for a while to avoid another spell.

We ascended the stairs and passed a number of closed doors until we finally stopped in front of one. 'You can lie down in here for a bit, Miss. This used to be Anna's room so you should find it most comfortable.'

'That is very kind of you Mr… Oh please forgive me but I do not know your name – what should I call you?'

'My name is Chapman, Louis Chapman.' Only when he gave his name did he establish eye contact. 'When you feel well enough, the Master has requested that you wash up and dress in something suitable for a night among society. You will find many nice things in Anna's old wardrobe that should fit you. Just ring for me if you need any assistance, though I am afraid we do not have a lady's-maid. We had no real need for them after Anna and Mrs Weir… after they were no longer here.'

'I assure you it is no trouble at all; I have become quite accustomed to dressing myself. Will my mother be accompanying us?'

'Mrs Maines is still attending to her duties I'm afraid. But the Master thought it would be agreeable for you to join him this evening, as you would otherwise be on you own.'

'I see, yes. Thank you, Mr Chapman, I shall call if I require anything,' I said, stepping into the room.

Chapman was gone and I stood examining the room that had once belonged to Mr Weir's daughter. How strange that seemed to me. In the centre of the room was an ornately carved wooden four-poster bed with thick damask bed curtains. Years of polishing had left the tiny carved angels softly worn around the edges. He must have loved his daughter very much for this room was the most beautiful room I had ever seen.

Filled with anticipation I walked over to the wardrobe. My mind could only imagine what lay behind such beauty. As I opened the doors, I gasped with exhilaration. Even as a child, I had not possessed such beautiful items.

I fumbled through the clothes in search of something suitable for the evening. It would have been useful to know where he was taking me – but somehow I knew the intrigue excited him. He preferred it that way.

The resentment I had felt that afternoon at the dressmaker's had subsided. I was now caught up by the allure of the numerous fabrics and colours I had to choose from. My eyes fixed upon the most gorgeous gown I had ever seen. It was one long piece of fabric, made of a luscious red taffeta, richer in colour than that of the finest red rose. Its only embellishment was a red satin ribbon fastened beneath the bust that gathered the fabric together and tied into a bow at the back.

I removed the gown from the wardrobe, placed it across the bed and then searched for a pair of matching shoes. Sure enough, I soon found a pair and tried them on to be sure they fitted. Their size could not have been more perfect. I wondered if the dress would fit as well. It did look to be the right size. I pulled at the ties that held me into my plain bluish-grey frock and let it drop to the ground. I stepped out of it and lifted up the red dress. It felt wrong to put something so pretty over such tattered and worn petticoats and undergarments and I made a mental note to search for replacements amongst Anna's things.

I pulled off my soiled layers and lifted the red dress up over my head. The silky fabric slid down over my bare skin and fell into place. I retied the ribbon at the back, which I had to undo to put on. I studied myself in the wardrobe mirrors – this would certainly do.

It was then that I thought I saw the reflection of someone standing in the doorway, but when I turned to look no one was there. I thought of calling for Mr Chapman but decided against it as I was meant to be having a rest. I was indeed feeling quite tired.

Having taken off the dress and placed it over the back of a chair, I climbed on to the large four-poster bed and buried myself deep under the white covers. I let my heavy eyelids drop and fell into the darkness of sleep.

CHAPTER 5

The sound of Mr Weir's voice woke me from my sleep. 'Rose...
darling wake up.'

Was I dreaming?

'What, where am I? What time is it?' I asked, trying to shake
off my confusion.

'You fell asleep. If we are going to make the ballet you really
must get dressed,' Mr Weir responded patiently. He was seated on
the edge of the bed staring down at me.

I was fully awake now. I felt refreshed and rested and could not
recall when I had last had such a sound sleep.

'I'll get dressed at once,' I said, propping myself up by my
elbows. My face grew red and hot as I remembered I had nothing
on beneath the covers. An unfamiliar sensation was now present
deep within my belly. 'Please, you must go...'

'Yes, of course.' His eyes wandered slowly over me, as if taking
in the image of me, before he turned away. 'It is most improper.
I did knock, but could not seem to rouse you. I should not have
entered. I have forgotten myself... Forgive me.' He removed
himself from the bed and proceeded towards the door. 'I shall be
waiting for you downstairs.'

Once he left the room, I pushed off the coverings and got out
of bed. Locating a pitcher of water and basin I quickly gave myself
a wash. When I was satisfied I was suitably clean, I opened the
wardrobe to search for a chemise and petticoats and to my surprise
they were right there in front of me. Curious... I did not recall
seeing them there before.

Once I was fully dressed, I sat in front of the dressing table and pulled out a small drawer and found within it some hairpins and red ribbon. I pinned back my curls as best I could away from my face then tied my locks with the red ribbon. Then came the final step. I put on the perfectly fitting shoes, left the room and made my way down the hall.

Mr Weir stood waiting for me at the bottom of the stairs. His upright posture formed a perfectly straight line from head to toe. In his outstretched hand, he was holding a small box tied with a red ribbon. His eyes wandered over me approvingly.

'I see you found something appropriate to wear. Red is my favourite colour, you know.' Giving me a little wink he handed me the box. 'Open it – I think you'll find it suits you well.' He took a step towards me, his presence once again overwhelming me. My heart beat rapidly.

'No, I think I will wait. May we go?' My eyes held his gaze firmly. Moments ago he had been seated beside me whilst I was in bed. How long had he watched me asleep? My cheeks once again grew warm; I did not wish to linger.

Taking another step forward he leaned forward and whispered in my ear, 'Whatever's the matter, Rose? You are absolutely trembling.' He brushed his hand softly down my arm, its fine hairs rising as he did so. I closed my eyes and inhaled. When I opened them he was no longer beside me and was walking towards the awaiting carriage. Reluctantly I followed.

Mr Weir and I sat on opposite sides of the carriage. The little box sat within my lap, my fingers fumbling with the soft red ribbon.

'Go on, open it!' he said, in a tone that indicated it was not so much a request as an order.

I laced my forefinger and thumb around one of the ends of the ribbon and pulled it towards me. Delicately I lifted off the lid and placed it down beside me. Within the box was a pair of long white gloves on top of which lay a ruby and diamond necklace. I removed the ring my father had given me on his deathbed, pulled on the gloves, and replaced the ring. As a rule I never removed it. The necklace was a perfect match to it and they both accessorised the dress I had chosen to wear perfectly. I wondered… had he chose rubies simply because he thought they suited me? Could he have somehow known what I would wear? It was then that I had the most alarming thought – had it been Mr Weir I had seen in the reflection earlier?

A gigantic smirk stretched across the width of Mr Weir's face. He knew what I was thinking. 'You are a beautiful young woman, Rose. There is really nothing to be ashamed or embarrassed about.'

'I beg your pardon?' Had he really just admitted to watching me dress? I felt my cheeks redden. 'Your behaviour towards me is completely inappropriate.' I looked away mortified. My heart was pounding fiercely. At first I felt as though it would explode from my chest, I was so full of anger and fear. But as we drove along, I grew calmer and then unexpectedly there was a flutter of something else, a feeling I did not recognise.

There was something about him, something that drew me in, a part of him I could not resist. It infuriated me that one man could have such a confusing effect on me.

We spent the remainder of our journey in silence. When we finally came to a stop underneath the grand portico, I was relieved to escape the confines of the carriage.

Taking my hand, Mr Weir led me through the crowd of people. As we stepped through the entrance of the Opera House, I was immediately enamoured by the beauty of the grand foyer.

Under the glow of the lamplight the whole space seemed to shimmer. The air was sweet with the perfume of freshly cut flowers. Never in my life had I beheld anything so beautiful.

The fanfare was sounding, indicating that the first act was about to begin. Mr Weir led me hurriedly up a series of stairwells whose steps were covered with red carpeting. With each turn I felt ever more disoriented.

Pulling back a thick red curtain, an usher directed us to our seats; we had a balcony box all to ourselves. The people below looked like miniatures scurrying into place amongst the rows of seats.

Mr Weir handed me a pair of golden binoculars and as the lights dimmed around us, I looked through them to see a picture-perfect stage being unveiled from behind the enormous plush red curtains.

My breath was taken away by the spectacular view that lay before me, and as I turned to share my enthusiasm, I remembered who accompanied me.

A few latecomers scurried to their seats and silence fell over the crowd as the orchestra began. The dream-like set sparkled in the brilliant candlelight. A brightness like daylight illuminated the stage, leaving only the wings cast in deep shadow. The scene was a courtyard in a city and in the centre was a tall podium.

The orchestra played a soft lulling melody that echoed eerily throughout the auditorium. One by one, five women dressed in white flowing gowns and with long lustrous blonde hair entered the stage. An air of innocence surrounded them as they began to dance around the courtyard as if hypnotised by the music. The music became more intense and they matched its quickening tempo.

There was a synthesised thunderclap and the illusion of day gave way to the illusion of night, as a long slender figure appeared on the podium. The figure was wearing a long black cloak with the hood pulled up over his head, concealing his face. Thunder sounded once more and the figure raised his arms above his head dropping the cloak to his feet.

The crowd gasped: the face and body were those of a young girl but on her back were two long black wings. Was she an angel? An archangel perhaps? Her hair was long and black and hung loose about her waist. She wore a black flowing gown, which was not of the current fashion, and her face was expressionless and cold.

She looked down upon the ladies in white and lowered her

arms. As she did so they kneeled before her. With the abrupt spreading of her wings the ladies' pure-white gowns and blonde flowing hair turned black.

They resumed their wild dance while the girl appeared to fly down from the podium to the stage. She joined in the dance, every so often lifting one of her companions lightly into the air. I was mesmerised.

The lights dimmed and the curtains came down for a scene change; I could hardly wait to see what would happen next. When the curtains reopened the stage had been transformed into a forest. I could feel the hairs on the back of my neck stand on end.

A young girl came running out on to the stage from the left. She was dressed in a pale-blue flowing gown and danced across the stage as if she were trying to escape. I could feel her terror as the music mimicked her fearful desperation.

A male dancer entered the stage and danced after her. They were in a chase, weaving in and out of the painted trees. My heart was pounding and I almost leapt forward with excitement when he finally caught her in his grasp. She struggled to get away but he threw her about the stage in a choreographed but violent manner.

Once he finally had her subdued he lowered her to the ground pushing her golden hair off her face and kissing her. I could not bear to watch and closed my eyes. A sudden change in the music made me open them again; standing before the couple was the winged girl in black, the one from the podium. The man staggered away from his prey. Her garments were torn. The girl in black approached him, spreading her wings about him.

I could not understand why he did not run. When she finally reached him she pulled his face down to hers and wrapped her wings around him. The wings completely enveloped him. When she opened them again, he lay lifeless on the stage floor with a pool of red liquid surrounding his unmoving head.

She turned and glided over to the young girl who still lay motionless. She kneeled down before her and lifted her into her arms. She spun them around and closed her wings around the girl. When she opened her wings once more, I was surprised to see the girl was not dead, but was dressed in black like the dancers in the previous scene. I did not feel the pity and fear I knew I should be feeling. In their stead was a feeling of longing and excitement.

When the curtains swept across for the intermission, the audience took a moment to collect themselves and then broke out into a round of roaring applause.

Overcome with emotion, I could not help but cry. I was absorbing the flow of emotions around me.

'It is wonderful to see you so moved, Rose. You are enjoying the ballet?' Mr Weir probed, handing me a handkerchief.

Wiping the tears from my eyes, I turned to him and was surprised to see him smiling. My stomach tingled unusually as if satisfied by his reaction. Though I did not understand it fully, it somehow, somewhere deep inside, made sense to me.

Placing my arm through his, he escorted me from the box and down the stairs into the main hall. I could barely think over the chatter of the swarm of people around me.

'Where are you taking me?' I asked.

'Home.'

'But it is not yet finished. Why are we leaving?'

He gave no reply and continued to lead me out of the Opera House.

We stood outside for a brief moment in silence before the carriage arrived. How had the driver known we were leaving early? Perhaps he had been instructed to wait near by?

I sat in silence for the entire length of the ride. His mood seemed once again sombre and contemplative. Something had obviously upset him.

When we arrived at my street he walked me to my door. 'Good night, Rose. I shall call on you again tomorrow.' He did not wait for me to accept his request to call on me. He just returned to his carriage and drove away.

Mother was still at the Weir residence. The house was silent and still. I was grateful for the solitude.

Removing my gloves I entered the bedroom. I felt out of place. My simple surroundings no longer comforted me.

I pulled out the hairpins one by one and dropped them on to my dressing table. Taking one end of the red ribbon in between my index finger and thumbs I unbound the remaining locks of copper hair.

Why had our evening been cut short? He certainly was a strange and confusing man.

Undressing I hung the gown in my wardrobe and climbed into bed. As my head settled into the softness of my pillow, I fell into a deep and dreamless slumber.

CHAPTER 6

Before long a new day had begun. As I began to stir, my eyes adjusting to the morning light, a faint figure appeared at the foot of my bed. A feeling of repulsion overcame me as the identity of the figure became clear. It was Mr Weir.

I froze – not knowing whether to scream or to cover myself first.

Noticing I was awake, he began to speak. 'Ah you are awake. Good. You seemed so peaceful... I did not want to disturb you.' He released his hands from the foot of my bed and placed them by his side.

I took a moment to collect myself. 'What are you doing here? Does my mother know you are here?'

'Your mother sent me. She did not get her duties done until late last night and spent the night in one of my vacant rooms. This morning she requested that I came to fetch you and bring you back to my house so that you would not be alone.' As he spoke his eyes wandered studiously over the delicate curves of my scantily clad figure.

Pulling the bed coverings firmly around me, I ordered him to leave my room.

Obediently he moved to leave, but as he did so he gripped the bottom corner of the bed sheet and dragged it slowly away from me as he walked towards the door. He opened the door, turning back to look upon me. A sideways smile stretched across his face, as if in approval. I shuddered.

Mr Weir stood outside the door as I dressed. I could not understand why Mother had not returned. It was not like her to work so long into the night. Perhaps she was just trying to make a good impression; after all, he was the first gentleman who had ever requested her services so personally.

I made no effort to dress well that day. I decided, too, to wear my hair pinned up, as I did not have the time to brush it out properly.

On our journey to Mr Weir's, I made a point of avoiding any long discussion with him. He seemed more content today, and not in his usually abrasive mood.

My thoughts turned to our encounter earlier; I saw the image of his crooked smile in my mind and I felt my lips curl at the memory. His influence was growing on me.

Reaching out my hand, I gently stroked his cheek.

He grabbed my wrist and removed it from his face. However, he did not let go and his squeeze grew tighter and tighter. The pain was incredible.

'Must you insist on teasing me so?' His grip loosened slightly but he still did not let go.

'You're hurting me. Please let go.' I could feel the moisture building in my eyes.

'It is you who hurts me, Rose.' His face had grown hard and his eyes were fixed on mine with all the intensity of a lion who had caught sight of his prey.

'I do not understand. How have I hurt you? I only wished to comfort you.'

'Do not play coy with me – I know exactly what you are up to. You're all the same – little Rose fair and innocent. Well, I won't fall for it. I know exactly what you are.'

Before I even realised we had arrived, and he was dragging me inside his house by my wrist and up the stairs. I feared my arm would be ripped from its socket, his grip upon it was so firm.

He flung me on to the floor of a room I had never been in before and shut the door behind us.

I needed to get out of there.

Quickly he advanced towards me and as I tried to leap to my

feet he grabbed me by the waist. I heard my dress tear under his foot as he lifted me by the arm and spun me around to face him.

His breath was hot and stale upon my face, his eyes full of rage. I wanted to scream out but I was too terrified to open my mouth. His face was so close to mine that I could see the black-and-grey stubble of his unshaven jaw.

I began to pound on his chest with my fists, struggling to get free. Yet this only intensified his anger. He raised his arm and slapped me so hard across the face that I was knocked backwards on to the floor.

I could not believe this was happening. I managed to stumble to my feet, but my head felt dizzy and confused. I needed to get out of there. I feared what would happen next.

Staggering towards the door I grasped the doorknob and turned it. It was locked. I was trapped. I felt the surge of tears rising from within me once again. I banged my hand hard against the door and tried to call out, but nothing came. The saltiness of my tears flooded into my gaping mouth. I sunk towards the ground and turned to face him.

He gave me a sideways smile and sat down on the edge of the bed.

'Well, we are in a bit of a predicament here, aren't we?' He slowly began removing his black leather gloves placing them down on the bed.

'Mr Weir, I beg of you,' I pleaded, tears running down my face. 'Just leave me alone.'

He started towards me again. I curled up into a ball against the door and cried out, hoping someone would hear us. No one came. He towered over me and reached down to pick me up. He threw me over his shoulder and then down on to the bed. I feared the worst. He hovered for a moment over me, with his hands on either side of my head.

'Please,' I begged almost inaudibly, before closing my eyes. When I opened them he was heading towards the door.

'Where are you going?' I called after him.

'I'm doing what you asked of me – leaving you alone.'

Having quickly unlocked the door he exited the room and slammed the door behind him. I heard the click of the lock.

'Why are you doing this? Don't leave me in here!' I shouted, trying to lift myself off the bed. My head throbbed: the excitement had taken its toll and I felt dizzy and weak.

As I heard his footsteps retreat down the hallway and descend the stairs, I began to feel calmer.

I evaluated the extent of my injuries. My arm was red and hot where he had grabbed me, my cheek felt sore and tender. I ran my fingers over the welt, the flesh burning at the slightest touch. My dress was torn at the hem where it had become trapped under his foot. I grabbed the material in my hand and closed my fingers around it, as if trying to will the fabric to mend, for the physical reminder of our altercation to vanish.

When I finally collected myself I took in my surroundings. This must certainly be Mr Weir's bedroom. I was lying on his bed. Regaining some of my strength I managed to lift myself into a seated position and ran my right hand softly over the bed curtains. They were dark red and heavily embroidered with yellow and white flowers. The bedding and the walls were also a deep red and a single armchair stood in front of a recently lit fire.

I went over to one of the windows and I drew back the curtain to look out. As I did, whirls of dust floated off of them. The sun was shining brightly into my eyes and I could feel its warmth embrace me, comforting me.

The window faced the street and as I looked down I saw Mr Weir enter his carriage and drive off. I felt relieved he was out of the house – for a little while at least. But I was still locked in here. I debated calling out to Mother or to Chapman. How would I explain? Surely I was partly to blame for what had transpired. No, it was best to simply wait for him to return. I imagined his mood would be improved and no more harm would come to me.

Light-headedness suddenly came over me so I headed back towards the bed. I needed to rest a moment.

As I lay down on Mr Weir's bed, I felt my mind drifting away from reality and off into the realm of dreams.

Once more, I was running through the forest, my eyes wet with tears, clouding my vision. Footsteps began to follow me. I fell down in front of a pond and looked back but could not make out the identity of the dark figure approaching. I could feel someone's breath on my neck.

I managed to stand and peer into the water before me. Here I saw Mr Weir's arms wrap around me, embracing me. His face was wet with blood. 'What have you done to me?' he asks, putting his hand over my mouth as I try to scream. 'You are one of them, Rose. You always have been.' And then he's gone and I am alone.

CHAPTER 7

I awoke to the loud crash of the door hitting the wall as Mr Weir entered the room. He was soaking wet from head to toe. How long had I been asleep for? It had not been raining when he had left.

He seemed to take no notice of me as he stumbled towards his armchair. I cowered on the bed as I watched him scoop another pile of coal on to the fire and pour himself a drink.

Despite his earlier treatment of me, I did not feel anger towards him. His treatment towards me was wrong, vile, but at least he had shown a glimpse of his true self. I had been right to distrust him.

Now sitting there, drenched in rain and shivering from the cold, he looked so harmless. Did he even remember I was there?

In the soft glow from the fire, I thought I saw my father sitting there and not Mr Weir. My father weak from the rain and looking so sick, as he had just before he died.

I lifted myself off the bed and walked towards him. I removed his wet coat and placed it down in front of the fire. He did not look at me, but instead took a long swig of his drink.

I kneeled before him and began to unlace his shoes, removing them one at a time and placing them beside his jacket. I saw that his wet black hair was plastered to his face, so I lifted my hand and gently moved it away from his eyes. He looked up at me. Within his eyes I saw a flicker of emotion behind the darkness. I unbuttoned and removed his shirt and then I placed a blanket around his pale freckled shoulders. He did not speak but let his appreciation of my attentions be felt.

I sat down in front of him and rested my head on his lap.

'You're not dead, are you? No, you cannot be for you are here with me.' I whispered to myself, wanting so much to believe that the illusion was real. I could feel his pain and knew he felt mine. The warmth of the fire comforted me and for a while I began to feel safe in his presence.

When Mr Weir's voice eventually broke the silence, I was sucked back into the reality of where I was and with whom.

'I know I cannot replace your father. Just as you cannot replace my Anna. All I want is to be happy, for *you* to be happy.' His voice was soft and sincere as he spoke to me.

Pushing me aside, he rose from his chair and walked over to his wardrobe. He opened its doors and retrieved a dry shirt. He shrugged the blanket off his shoulders; it fell to the floor, revealing his pale bare chest. I quickly changed the direction of my gaze. Out of the corner of my eye I saw him retrieve a dry pair of trousers and begin to unfasten the wet ones. I closed my eyes to avoid seeing anything further. He was not unpleasant to look at, but the free manner in which he behaved made me uncomfortable.

His footsteps approached the door and so I turned to see what he was doing. 'I had best get you back home.' Not waiting, he began to head down the hallway.

Gathering up any loose strands of hair, I pinned them back into place. I took out one of the hairpins and temporarily fastened the rip in my dress. Descending the stairs, I joined Mr Weir and we headed out into the darkness of an overcast afternoon.

The air was moist and thick from the rain that had momentarily ceased. There was no carriage waiting and as Mr Weir swung open the iron gate and continued down the street on foot, I followed.

As we walked, several men staggered past, either on their way home from a public house or on to the next. What kind of men spent their afternoons in such places? Certainly not respectable ones.

Mr Weir's long black cloak clung to his slender figure as he walked, making him look taller than he actually was.

My stomach ached. I had not eaten since the day before.

'Forgive me, Rose, you must be ravenous. I should take you somewhere to eat,' he said suddenly, as if the thought had just occurred to him. He had a way of addressing my thoughts without me actually speaking them.

'I am a bit hungry, yes. But I fear it will be difficult to find anywhere that will accept me dressed like this.' I said, holding up the torn section of my dress. I had misplaced my cloak and bonnet somewhere. I could not recall where. I looked a mess.

'Valid point. That tear is my doing. Let me make it up to you. I know a good chop-house where they will not turn us away. Come.'

Following him, he led me towards the establishment he spoke of. Once we arrived, we entered and sat at a small wooden table on two mismatched chairs.

Mr Weir flagged someone's attention. 'Freddie, my dear boy, nice to see you. How's about you fetch the lady and I two Scotch sirloins and a pint of bitter.' It was strange to see him behave so comfortably and at apparent ease.

'Sure thing, Oli. I'll have some roasted up for yous nice and tasty on the old fire,' the man said, giving Mr Weir a jovial pat on the back.

'Oli?' I asked, curiously.

'Yes, Rose. My name is Oliver. You are welcome to address me as such. All this "Mr Weir" business is so dreadfully formal.'

He gave me a wink and took a sip of his beer, which had been placed down in front of him. With the back of his hand he wiped away a layer of foam from the top of his lip.

'If it is all the same to you … I'd rather not. Things are indecent enough already – surely we should hold on to some level of propriety.'

'What nonsense! Why must we behave as we are expected to? Everyone is so obsessed with all these little rules – "You must do this", "You mustn't do that." It's all so boring – not in the least bit fun!' Mr Weir pounded his fist on the table, drawing the attention of a couple of other patrons, who pretended not to notice.

'One cannot simply do as one pleases. These "little rules", as you call them, protect us from immoral behaviour. I would rather be proper and virtuous in the eyes of God, Sir, than succumb to sin.'

'Do you really believe that, Rose? That it is God's plan for us to be virtuous.' Mr Weir leaned forward into the table and looked at me intently.

'It is not a matter of belief, Sir – this is what the Scriptures teach us. The urge to sin is deep within us. Eve gave into her temptation by biting into the flesh of the forbidden fruit. She serves as a lesson to us all. Temptation is all around and it is our duty to God to remain strong and to be ever alert.'

'Rose, I hardly think calling me by my Christian name will send you plummeting down into the inferno.' He laughed and leaned back into his chair, rocking it onto its hind two legs.

'You find me silly.' I smiled. His laugh was infectious and I began to laugh with him.

Our food arrived and we ate in silence. Despite my moment of good humour I still felt cautious around him. He was clearly not a God-fearing man and that could be very dangerous.

After we finished eating, he walked me the remainder of the journey home. When we arrived at my door I turned to bid him goodnight.

'Rose, listen, I am truly sorry about earlier. I lost my temper. I really wish us to be friends and hope that you will find it within you to forgive me,' he said, taking my hand in his.

'Think of it no more. It is already forgotten.' I assured him and rose onto my tiptoes to give him a gentle kiss on his cheek. 'Goodnight, Oliver,' I said, smiling as the sound of his name passed my lips.

'Goodnight, fair Rose,' he replied, before departing into the night.

When I entered the house, I could feel the heat of the fire on my face. Mother was sound asleep in her armchair. Her long slender figure looked frail and her greying hair outlined her once-youthful face. My poor dear mother, how rapidly she had aged since entering service.

Not wishing to wake her, I crept quietly into my room. I lit a candle, changed into my nightshift and sat in front of my mirror. In the pale glow of the candlelight I began to brush out my hair. As the flame grew higher I noticed a large bruise on my face.

How would I explain this to Mother? What would I say? I could tell her the truth, but she might not believe me. Would she side with me over her employer? It had already been several months since her last position and we needed the income to keep our lodgings.

I went to bed that night with a crisis of conscience. The tingling of my bruises troubled me. I needed to stay away from him. He was not to be trusted. As I closed my eyes I thought I saw his face and he was smiling crookedly at me the way he often did. His hand reached up and brushed the hair from his eyes. They were warm and inviting.

Perhaps it was not that I did not trust him that worried me. Perhaps it was that I knew I did not trust myself.

CHAPTER 8

The next day I was relieved to wake to an empty apartment. The kitchen was cool and damp. I lit the cooker to boil some water for tea. I stood over it for a moment taking in the heat. As I was placing the pot on, I noticed something on Mother's chair. I walked over to get a closer look. It was a red rose accompanied by a letter addressed to me.

Opening it I read the contents: *Be sober, be vigilant; because your adversary the devil, as a roaring lion, walketh about, seeking whom he may devour – 1 Peter 5:8.*

I recognised the passage. But why had it been left for me?

The boiling of the kettle pulled me from my thoughts. Mother had left some fresh bread out. Beside it was another piece of paper, written in Mother's handwriting. It was only an address with instructions to go to it. I tucked both pieces of paper into my pocket and continued with my morning routine.

When I was finally ready to start the day I pushed open the front door. A wave of fresh air washed over my face. The rain appeared to be holding off for the time being, but the day was cool and damp. Avoiding the main streets as much as possible, I hurried towards my destination. The rat-infested alleys were filled with the usual street urchins and prostitutes. They did not bother with me, though. I had passed through these streets many times before and was quite familiar with them. Not that this made me any less afraid, just more accustomed to their presence.

I made my way west easily and in good time. As I weaved through the narrow streets, I found myself wondering what Mr Weir was doing today.

Walking quite quickly now, I took my mother's note from my pocket and found that I was only a short distance from my destination. Soon the address on the paper matched the number of the house that stood in front of me. I rapped lightly on the door and waited patiently for an answer. I could hear rustling from within and then the fumbling of the lock being unlatched. A rather portly man opened the door and, before I could utter a word, he stretched out his oversized arm and pulled me within.

Slamming the door behind us he stood aside. The tiny stairway ahead creaked softly as a thin handsome man proceeded down them two steps at a time.

He looked me up and down and then began to address me.

'You must be Rose. Lovely, lovely,' he grinned. 'I have heard quite a bit about you, darling. So nice, so nice to have you here.' Pausing for a moment, he brushed away a thick lock of blond hair that had fallen across his brow and licked his pink dry lips. 'Well, I shan't keep you waiting, my dear. Here is the correspondence.'

He shoved a white envelope into my hands and returned up the stairs in the same fashion as before. When he reached the top step he stopped and turned. 'You know, you are a lot prettier than I thought you'd be. Oliver sure knows how to pick them,' he chuckled. 'Be careful, love. He's a bit of a wild one.'

I was ushered out of the house in a state of confusion. Why had Mr Weir spoken of me to this man? What place was it of his to speak of me at all? I was determined to find the underlying cause of this misunderstanding when next we spoke.

I looked at the address on the envelope and a feeling of dread came over me. I would be confronting Mr Weir sooner than expected: the letter was addressed to him.

While walking I went over the best way to approach Mr Weir. He was so unpredictable and I rather wished to avoid a repeat of the day before. My approach would have to be determined when I saw him; only then would I be able to tell what mood he was in, and the level of his patience.

When I finally arrived, Chapman answered the door and told me that Mr Weir was in the garden. He showed me to a side door and I followed a path around the house.

I stopped in my tracks as I turned a corner into the garden. Mother was sitting on a small stone bench next to Mr Weir, her pale hands enwrapped in his snakelike fingers. She was laughing loudly at something he had said. I felt ill. A mixture of protectiveness and jealousy.

Mr Weir stood and placed a kiss on her hand then headed towards the house. I could not bring my body to move. My heart beat louder as his footsteps neared.

Turning the corner, he saw me.

'Ah, Rose,' he said with a smile, 'to what honour do I deserve such an unexpected but delightful surprise?' He placed a hand against the wall on either side of me.

My voice caught in my throat and I could not reply.

'Perhaps you brought the letter from my colleague, Mr Stead? Or did you simply miss me?' He reached his hand into my pocket and retrieved his letter. 'Letter it is,' he said before heading inside.

I regained my composure and followed him inside. He entered his study and retrieved a metal letter opener from his desk, before taking a seat in front of the fire. He broke the seal with one swift swipe of the blade and quickly read what it said before placing it on the small table beside him.

He motioned for me to sit down in the vacant chair opposite him. His face had become hard and unamused, his playful smile no longer present. I dared not disobey.

He stared blankly at me for some time, before speaking. 'Did you get my note? It is my favourite passage in the Bible, you know.'

I could tell he was eager for a response so I answered without hesitation. 'I received it, yes. Although I cannot say I fully comprehended the meaning behind it.'

'Our little chat yesterday about good and evil and of temptation got me thinking. That passage came to mind.' Mr Weir reached into his pocket and pulled out a shiny silver case. He lit a cigarette and continued: 'How can one be certain which is which?'

'You mean… How can we be certain what is good and what is evil?' I asked to be sure I had not misunderstood the question.

'Yes, Rose, that is precisely what I mean. How can a mere mortal be expected to tell the difference between the divine wonders of God and the temptations of evil? Surely, the devil would make his temptations wondrous and beautiful so as to trick us into desiring them.'

'That is what the commandments are for, to guide us. God has provided us with a very clear set of rules to abide by and these rules are enforced by the law.' I could not understand why he was pressing the matter so. 'Are you having a crisis of faith, Mr Weir?'

He laughed. 'No Rose. My faith is perfectly intact. I simply wished to know your views on the subject of temptation. The idea troubles me so.'

His words brought to mind my earlier interactions with Mr Stead. 'May I ask what you said to your colleague about me? He seemed to be under the impression that there was something perhaps inappropriate about the nature of our acquaintance,' I asked, assuming now was as good a time as any to raise the subject.

'Oh pish posh. That William is an eccentric young fellow with a habit of exaggerating the truth. You toss a lady's name around once or twice and he thinks things are what they are not. I assure you I said nothing inappropriate about you, Rose, and I will be sure to clarify the matter when I next see him.'

Whether he was speaking the truth, I could not tell; I was not sure if he ever spoke the truth. I worried for my mother bending to the charms of such a cleverly deceitful man. 'So what did you and my mother have to speak about that was so amusing?'

'So full of questions today, dear one. If you must know, we were speaking of your living arrangements. I wish for you both to come live here for a while. There is more than enough room here and it simply does not make sense for her to be travelling back and forth each day. Of course, it is entirely up to her and she plans to discuss it with you before giving me her decision.'

'We manage quite well on our own. Thank you! And have done so for many years,' I retorted. I could not bear the thought of living under the same roof as him.

His sharp black eyes stung me with their glare. 'That is for the two of you to discuss, but I would be lying if I said I did not hope that her answer would be yes.' Butting out his cigarette he stood and exhaled. A cloud of smoke veiled his face.

Our brief conversation was over. He gave every indication of wishing me to leave, and as I had nothing further to say to him I saw myself out.

As I stepped out into the cool air, I felt ill. I could not imagine having to wake up under the same roof as that man every day.

What would become of me if Mother agreed to us living there? I could not decipher what exactly he felt for me, but to think there was not more to his intentions than he led on would be foolish.

My step had quickened into a run and my heart was pumping loudly within my chest. Large drops of rain began to moisten my face. Yet I had no desire to seek shelter. My head began to throb and everything around me began to spin. There was a loud thump as my body hit the ground and darkness overtook me.

When I regained consciousness moments later Mr Weir was calling my name. I was not afraid. He was gently stroking my face and I felt safe there with him. The rain was pouring down so heavily upon us, it was as if it wished to wash us away.

'You are lucky I followed you, Rose. You seem to be rather prone to fainting. Perhaps we should have a doctor take a look at you?' As I looked into his eyes I did not see anger or deceit, only the immense care he took of me.

I reached up and returned the gesture by caressing his cheek in gratitude. He smiled down at me with his cold bluish lips and lifted me into his long slender arms. As he walked, I began to feel very weak again and closed my eyes. I listened to the hypnotic rhythm of his shoes clicking on the pavement and drifted into sleep.

CHAPTER 9

I was roused into consciousness by a gentle knocking. My eyes opened slowly one by one and my surroundings began to take shape beneath the spidery veil of fluttering lashes. I was back in Mr Weir's bedroom.

Groggily I called out for whomever it was to enter. Mr Weir came into the room carrying a silver tray.

'I took the liberty of fetching you tea and some dry clothing to wear,' he said, closing the door behind him.

I peeked under the blanket: my wet clothing had been removed but to my relief I was still wearing my chemise.

Mr Weir carefully placed the tray down on the bed.

'Here. Put these on,' he instructed, handing me the dry clothing. 'You will catch a chill if you stay in that much longer.'

I made a gesture with my hand for him to turn around. With an amused smile he obeyed and I made the switch of garments, quickly covering myself back up with the bedding.

'You may turn around now,' I instructed, before taking a mouthful of soup.

He took a seat in front of the fire. 'What was it that you were running from this time, Rose?' he asked, not removing his eyes from the dancing flames.

What had I been running from? 'To be honest, I am not really sure. Perhaps I was running from nothing at all. But maybe I was in fact running from myself.' I took a sip of tea and placed the cup back on to the tray. I could feel the liquid burning its way down my throat into my belly, but I did not mind the momentary discomfort for it was warming and that felt nice.

Mr Weir let out a low rumbling chuckle. 'From yourself? Why I have never heard a lady speak in such a way. You mean to say you knew not why or from what you were running?'

'It is only that my thoughts become so confused when I am around you. I begin to question how it is that I am meant to behave, or what I should say. You provoke such conflict within me. The way you speak to me, the questions you ask… it makes me afraid.'

'Afraid? Rose, could it be that what you really fear is the thought of actually enjoying my company? Are you afraid of how that makes you feel, of what you might want to happen between us?'

'No, that is not true at all Mr Weir.' I looked away. I felt his eyes on me. But when I looked up he was still staring into the fire. I sighed. 'And yet I have no choice but to share your company.'

'Is that so?'

'Yes, and what's worse is that I find myself thinking of you when we are apart. Why is it that I cannot simply walk out that door right now and never think of you again?' I pushed the tray off of my lap, I began to weep, wiping away the tears as they fell. 'Why will you not look at me? Why do you sit and stare at those flames as if they provided all the answers? Look at me!'

He turned his face towards me. His eyes were full of sadness and pain, not the anger that I was expecting. Was this the effect of my words? Or was it something else that troubled him?

I wanted to leave yet I also wanted to be closer to him, to comfort him. Climbing from the bed I went to him. I curled myself on to his lap and rested my head on his chest. 'Why do we argue so? Why must we hate each other?'

'Rose, I do not hate you. All I want is for you to give me a chance, for you to love me. I would do anything to make that so, to win your affections.'

'Oliver, I am not some prize to be won. Will you not accept that I will never love you, *could* never love you?' I got up and

48

headed towards the door. 'Please do not follow me.' I placed my hand on the doorknob and turned – it was locked.

'Did you really think I would let you leave?' He stood and walked towards me.

'I am grateful for your help earlier but you have no right to keep me here. Please just let me go.' I was afraid. He was suddenly in one of his moods.

As he approached me I buckled down into a ball. He grabbed me by the hair, lifted me to my feet and dragged me towards the window. He pulled back the curtain and stayed behind me. 'See those people down below rushing around? Do you not ever see them as cattle mindlessly going about their worthless lives? You and I are not like them, Rose, because we understand the world and our place in it. I take what I want, darling, and I do not want the mindless cow that understands nothing. I want the sheep, the innocent little sheep that can sense when she is in danger of being devoured by the lion. You, my dear Rose, are that sheep, whether you like it or not. You may tread carefully watching every step you take but sometimes that is not enough and eventually you will be swept off those feet of yours only to fall into my waiting arms.'

'Oliver, please release me.' I could feel his hot breath on the back of my neck and his hands tightening around my waist pulling me in closer to him.

'I cannot do that, Rose. You must learn to behave or risk the consequences. Is that understood?' He pushed against me, wrapping his fingers around my throat. 'I said: is that understood?' He spun me round so I was now facing him.

'I understand not a word. You speak nonsense!' I cried, slapping him across the face.

'Why must you test my patience?' he said. He kept his hand firmly on my throat and rubbed my cheek with his free hand. 'You have no idea what I am capable of, my dear, and you would be wise to remember your place.'

'I would rather die than have to spend another moment with

you.' I struggled to free myself from his grasp but his fingers tightened further around my neck. My breath was beginning to slow and my body began to feel tingly all over. I looked into his cold dark eyes. They were empty, as if the taking of a life meant nothing to him. Just as I was about to lose consciousness, when I thought that my pathetic life had finally reached its culmination, he let go.

With relief I fell to my knees and began to gasp for air.

'Next time you say you would rather die, you had better mean it.' He closed the curtain with a swift jerk and returned to his chair, lighting a cigarette.

Regaining my strength, I got up and moved towards him. 'I would rather die than be yours, so next time do us both a favour and do not let go.'

'That is what I love about you, Rose. You are so strong-willed, so feisty, like a wild unbroken horse...' he laughed mockingly, '...just begging to be broken.'

'You speak of love but you are not capable of love. No one as vile as you could ever love. That is why your wife left you, not because of your constant absence, which I am certain she must have considered a blessing, but because you were incapable of really loving her. I bet you were cruel to your wife – to your daughter! – just as you are cruel to me.'

He stopped laughing and was quick to defend himself. 'I loved Anna and I was never cruel to her. She was my life, my everything. Isabel knew that, yet she still took her from me.'

'And your wife – did you ever truly love her?'

'Of course I did. I am capable of love, Rose. Life just never gave me another chance to try.' He paused, looking towards me. 'That is until I met you.'

'How could you speak of such things? We barely know each other and I am half your age! I could never love you!' I cried. I could not bear the thought of any sort of love evolving between the two of us.

'If you despise me so much, why have you not refused to see me? You could easily inform your mother of all that has transpired between us but you do not. Are you afraid that she will not believe you? That she would take my word over her own daughter?' He smiled at me.

I could feel the rage building inside of me. 'How dare you say that! My mother loves me and would never take your word over mine.' Before I could restrain myself, I was charging towards him lashing out as his face. A thin trickle of blood began to flow from where I caught his cheek with my ring.

He soon overpowered me and threw me to the ground, pinning my hands to the floor beneath his. The stench of his breath was indescribable and as he began to speak, the smell became unbearable. 'Look what you've done. Why do you insist on making me hurt you? I am not a violent man, yet whenever I am with you I seem to lose control.'

I kept silent, fearing what might become of me if I did not.

He still had me pinned to the ground. 'Now that I have your undivided attention, perhaps we might discuss the matter of you and your mother coming to live with me,' he said, taking the opportunity to broach our earlier conversation.

'Never!' I screamed.

'Listen to me, Rose, you are going to speak with your mother tomorrow and let her know that you and I have come to an agreement and that you would be delighted to come to live here. If you are clever, which I believe you are, you will not say otherwise.' I could feel his hands tighten around my wrists and the look in his eyes gave me warning not to utter a word of further protest. 'Now I think we are quite finished with this discussion.'

He brushed his lips against mine. I closed my eyes tight, hoping to push the vision of his face out of my mind. 'Let's get you home before I do something we shall both regret,' he said, lifting me to my feet.

He unlocked the door and led me out of the room. Either no

one else was in or these walls were very thick, for surely someone would have overheard our confrontation and come to see what was the matter.

As we approached the stairs I could hear Chapman down below. Perhaps he had learned to stay out of Mr Weir's private affairs?

As we descended the stairs, a look of surprise came over him. 'Master, what in heavens has happened to your face? Is the lady all right?'

'We are both fine, Louis. We seem to have a rather large rat on the loose upstairs. I and it had a bit of an altercation and then it ran off. If you could see that it is got rid of, I would be most grateful.'

Surely, Chapman did not believe such lies but it was not his place to confront his master and Mr Weir knew this.

'Of course, of course.'

'I will be escorting Rose home now. Could you fetch her a cloak or something a bit warmer to wear?'

Chapman nodded his head in compliance. 'I shall find the girl something immediately, Sir.'

Why could I not be stronger and speak out? Was he right? Did I care for him? I shook my head. It was not possible. How could the others not see through his facade, not see him for who he really was? I needed to get out of there, away from him. I found myself passing over the threshold and through the iron gate in a daze.

Mr Weir called after me, but he did not follow. Had he really meant the things he said? Did he really love me?

What was I to do? I had always felt as though I was a burden to my mother. We had never been that affectionate towards one another, especially after Father died. I often wondered whether, if she had not had to care for me, her life would have been easier, better. Perhaps she would have remarried.

I saw the way she looked at Mr Weir. If only it were not the loathsome Mr Oliver Weir who had rekindled such feelings in her. If only she could see him for what he truly was.

CHAPTER 10

Standing before our front door I took a deep breath and entered into the darkness. I fumbled to find a lamp then light flooded the empty room.

I moved across the room and set the lamp down on the mantle of the fireplace. I was still shaking from the cold as I lit the fire. The blaze began to rise and a blanket of heat enveloped me.

I had spent many a night crouched in front of this cosy little fire. Mother often slept out here now. She used to sleep with me, but stopped after she began working such long hours.

I saw the rose Mr Weir had left for me earlier that day. I picked it up and inhaled its sweet scent before throwing it into the fire. I watched each scarlet petal slowly begin to ignite. I knew I now belonged to him.

I felt tired and numb. I could no longer struggle against him. Not while Mother remained so infatuated with him. My only hope was that once we were all together constantly he would no longer be able to hide his true self.

When Mother returned home that evening, I was asleep in her chair. She woke me gently and asked if we could speak.

Fidgeting nervously with the folds of her uniform, she told me of Mr Weir's offer and how she planned to accept. The words did not come easy to her; she had gone so long without accepting the aid of others.

I nodded my agreement, knowing that in doing so I had just given consent to my own suffering. A wave of relief seemed to come over her. She knew I would not approve, but her desire to be near to him overpowered her otherwise independent and self-sufficient nature. Her happiness radiated from beneath her sallow skin.

For the next three days I did not see Mr Weir at all. I spent my last days of solitude gathering up the few belongings we had while Mother was kept busy with her duties. When the day arrived on which we were to move house, I felt that I had prepared myself for my fate as best I could.

Mr Weir was sending someone to fetch our things after tea and I decided to take advantage of what was a rare sunny day and go for a walk. I began to walk north and, although I was heading towards no particular destination, I felt guided, as if an invisible force steered me.

The sky was clear and bright but the chaotic world around me did not seem to slow.

His footsteps had become known to me a while back but I could not be certain he was still following. What was his fascination with me? I could not understand why he wanted me near to him. There was nothing I could offer him as a companion; as a woman my views were considered limited but he seemed interested in all I had to say, as if my opinion mattered a great deal to him.

As I turned the next corner, his carriage reared to a halt beside me. 'Ah, Rose, it is a pleasure to see you. It is much too busy a day to waste frolicking about. Get in and we shall have a bite to eat.'

When had he gave up his pursuit by foot and hailed a driver?

'Thank you for the offer, Oliver, but if it pleases you I'd rather continue alone.'

Walking briskly away, I heard him exit the carriage and approach from behind.

Grabbing my arm, he pulled me towards him.

'Apologies, my dear, we seem to have a bit of a misunderstanding – that was not a request. If you are going to live under my roof, you must become accustomed to keeping my company, Rose.' I obeyed and reaching his arm out the window he tapped the side to signal the driver to move on. 'I cannot express how happy I was to hear that you had agreed to our little arrangement,' he grinned.

'I hardly had a choice in the matter – you made that very clear to me the other day,' I responded coldly.

He snorted. 'You could have told her the truth about our little scuffle, but you did not. Is this because deep inside you feel the same need and longing for me that I feel for you?' He leaned back into the corner of the carriage opposite me.

The depth of his delusion was absurd and made me begin to laugh out loud.

'What, may I ask, do you find so amusing?' His face had turned crimson, not unlike that of the carriage's interior.

My laughter had now almost reached the point of hysteria.

'Stop it! Please just stop laughing. I warn you – STOP!' He grabbed me by my hair and pulled me close, placing his hand tightly over my mouth. I felt the roughness of his fingers as they pushed painfully against my lips.

My body seized up and my laughter stopped. I bit down on his fingers, desperate to be free from his painful grasp.

Showing no sign of pain, he did not remove his hand. 'Did you honestly think a pathetic little bite could harm me? You did not even draw blood.' He grimaced as he removed his hand from my mouth and slid it down around my waist.

'Get your hands off me!' I snapped.

'You can't blame me for wanting you close, Rose. Why do you fight me so?' His arm wrapped tighter around me. 'Do you not want life to be easier? It could be, if you just let it.' With his free hand he caressed my neck and pulled me close to him.

My heart raced, but I was not afraid. I wanted to push him away, to free myself, but I could not will my body to move. Something in the way he looked at me set my heart afire. I knew it was wrong – not because he was twice my age, not because in the eyes of God he was still a married man, but because I knew that, if I did not stop him – if I could not – it would be my undoing.

Leaning in towards me, he let his lips caress against mine. They felt warm and soft. He kissed me gently; I did not pull away. The pressure of his lips against mine intensified. An unfamiliar sensation grew in the bottom of my belly.

Staring up into his dark-brown eyes, I saw within them a gentleness, a kindness that had never been there before.

My lips quivered as he pulled away. Closing my eyes I could feel the building reservoir of tears spill over. 'You shall be the ruin of me.'

The wheels spun beneath us, hitting the ground hypnotically. I leaned into his chest and rested my head. I could feel my heart slowing down to the same tempo as the turning of the wheels.

Gazing out the carriage window I watched as we passed the borders of the city and entered its outskirts. Why were we going this way?

As we turned into a side road, familiarity overwhelmed me and I ordered the driver to halt. I pushed open the door and leapt out.

Mr Weir called after me but his voice faded into the billowing wind as I moved forward with great speed.

The sky was still clear but I could feel the cool tingle of rain against my skin. Everything seemed so familiar yet I could not recall having ever taken this road before.

Further down the road a dark figure approached. As the figure drew near I could see it was a man. He was staggering towards me. He was crying out for help. His legs gave way and he crashed face first into the ground before me.

I knelt down beside him and turned his body over to face me. I screamed with shock and disbelief at what I saw. There before me lay my father covered in blood, wounded but very much alive. I wrapped my arms around him and begged him to wake up.

Responding to my voice, his eyes fluttered open. His lips began to move but no words could be heard. I leaned in closer, bringing my ear close to his lips. 'It was her... She did this to me.'

I did not understand, 'Who? Who did this?'

But before he could respond he disappeared as miraculously as he had appeared and I was left sitting at the side of the road alone with tears streaming down my face. My hands were trembling.

'Rose, what in heavens are you doing?' Mr Weir asked. 'Come, we must not let anyone see you on the side of the road like this.' He helped me up then led me back into the carriage.

I felt as though I was losing my grip on reality; nothing made sense to me anymore.

'What did you see, Rose?'

'Nothing, I saw nothing. I was feeling ill and needed some air, that's all. Really, please do not question me any further on the matter.'

'Very well, Rose. I will not raise the subject again but I do believe you saw something and it obviously upset you.'

'You are mistaken.'

'You saw your father, didn't you? Wasn't that the same road his carriage got stuck on six years ago?'

'I asked you not to press me! How could I possibly know that? Do you really think they would tell a nine-year-old girl such things?' My mind was spinning. Could he be right? 'How is it that you know what I do not?'

'It was in the papers – surely your mother kept a copy?'

'And why would she keep such a thing? Do you not think his death was painful enough for her, for us, that she would wish to keep a keepsake?' I could not recall having ever seen an article in the paper.

'I'm sorry. You're right. It was silly of me to think such a thing. I trust you're feeling better?'

'Quite, please just let me close my eyes for a moment.' I leaned back and momentarily shut out the world around me. The vision of my father haunted me. Never before had I seen him look so afraid. Had I really glimpsed into the past?

The carriage shortly pulled to a halt in front of Mr Weir's

house. 'Welcome to your new home, Rose,' he said, extending his hand towards me.

I accepted his arm then followed him as he led me towards the familiar black door. His shadow cast over me, enveloping me in its darkness. I was not scared. I was home. In that moment I knew this was exactly where I was meant to be.

CHAPTER 11

Mr Weir was not at home much the first three weeks after Mother and I moved in. He had been called away for business somewhere in the Midlands and I was relieved by his temporary absence.

Mother kept busy with her duties around the house and I unpacked what little belongings we had. While Mr Weir was away, Chapman ensured that we had everything we required and for the first time in as long as I could recall I wanted for nothing.

My new life was one of solitude, of stasis. I missed the hustle and bustle of the East End. The familiarity. There were no errands for me to run, or washing to do, nothing needed mending or sorting out. I was not expected to be anywhere and no visitors called. Not that I expected them to. It had been many years since I had any true companions. I was too old to play and yet not in a position to attend the social engagements girls of my age and class were often invited to.

Giving into the call to be still, I picked up the copy of *Jane Eyre* Mr Weir had lent me, wrapped a shawl around my shoulders and went into the garden.

The sun shone brightly and the birds sang their sweet songs bringing to life the dull bare surroundings. The garden lay dormant, asleep under the spell of the approaching winter. Beyond the grey I could almost sense its secret beauty, lying in wait for spring to come and rouse it once again.

I inhaled deeply. The cool air tickled the insides of my nose. It smelled fresh. It smelt of freedom.

I saw a disorderly stone path through the sparse shrubbery and walked along it, following its lines as they swayed in and out. I sat on a stone bench in front of a moss-covered fountain and opened my book. I glanced over the first line: *There was no possibility of taking a walk that day.* The words were simple yet beautiful. I read on, taking in each sentence as if it were a line of poetry.

I ran my finger over the page, reading aloud the beginning of the next paragraph. *I was glad of it; I never liked long walks, especially on chilly afternoons: dreadful to me was the coming home in the raw twilight, with nipped fingers and toes.*

I closed my eyes and let the sun's warm embrace fill every ounce of me. I was grateful for a rare clear November day, a day where I could walk and just be at peace. I felt humbled.

The sound of a twig snapping under foot roused me from my sedate state.

'Who's there?' I called out.

I stood and scanned the garden. No one was there, but my attention was drawn to a bit of red amongst the otherwise monochrome landscape. I placed my book down on the bench, careful not to lose my page and walked towards it.

Within the tangle of a dormant rose bush had bloomed a single red rose. Reaching out I caressed its silky petals before snapping it free within my fingers. A thorn pierced my flesh, causing me to drop the flower. A small bead of blood was forming on the tip of my finger. I walked towards the fountain and let the blood trickle down into the pool of water.

Each droplet that hit the water caused a tiny circular ripple, and watching them my mind began to whirl. Flash after flash, segments of my dream appeared before me right here in my waking world. Forest, rose, blood, water, water, blood, rose, darkness. I could feel my body sinking beneath me and then eyes... eyes on me, watching.

I reached up, grabbing on to the edge of the fountain and pulled myself up. I began to weave through the garden searching for the intruder. Light-headed I stumbled and reached out for a nearby tree... anything to keep me upright. My hand grasped at something soft, malleable, an arm. My heart stopped.

'When did you return?' I asked.

Mr Weir stood before me, his face full of confused concern. 'I have only just. Do you feel poorly?'

'A bit light-headed but it passes. Please, I must sit down.'

Sliding his arm under my shoulder, he helped me towards the bench. 'Will you not confide in me, Rose? What is it that excites you so?'

'It is really none of your concern. You mustn't worry yourself.'

'But I do worry. I have seen the way your mind wanders. Even in your sleep your dreams trouble you.' We were now seated with his hands wrapped tightly around mine.

How could he possibly know about my dreams? I never spoke a word about them to anyone.

'You talk in your sleep, Rose. I have heard you call out, felt your heartbeat quicken. What is it that causes you such fear?'

'You do,' I said timidly.

'I do? You dream of me?'

'Sometimes, yes.' Why was I telling him this? What good would it do?

'And I frighten you?'

'Yes.' I pulled my hands away from him and concealed my face. I could not bear to look at him. 'Oliver, please. Forget I said anything.'

'Your words cut through me. I have invited you into my home and yet you still refuse to show me any kindness.' His voice was harsh and angry.

'Invited me? No, you insisted.' Removing my hands I gathered the courage to look upon his face. His brow was furrowed. His jaw clenched.

'Only because I wanted what was best for you and your lousy wench of a mother.'

'Insult me all you wish but do not speak ill of my mother. She has done nothing but worship you from the day you walked into our home. Are you so vile that you cannot even appreciate all that she has done for you?'

'I may not care for her as I care for you but I do appreciate her,' he said, his face softening a little.

'Why then do you deceive her so? If you do not care for her, then please, for pity's sake, do not act as though you do,' I begged, feeling the tears rush to my eyes.

'Is pity what possesses you to obey her every wish and keep secrets from her? If you cannot be truthful to your own mother, then why should I?' He stood and turned his back to me.

'The only secrets I keep are yours, and I keep them only because I know to share them with her would break her heart.' The tears began to spill over from my eyes as I continued. 'I simply cannot comprehend your justification for such false pursuit of her.'

Turning, he grabbed my hand and led me towards the fountain. He wrapped his arms around me and stood behind me. 'Look at your reflection, Rose. Can you not see what a beautiful young lady you have become? Do you think that time stopped when your father died? You are no longer a child of nine, Rose.'

'Why do you speak such things to me?' I tried to pull away but his grip was too strong.

'You and I we are meant to be together; from the moment I met you I knew such was true.'

'Oliver, from the moment I saw you I have despised you. Is that not reason enough for you to stop this endless pursuit of me, to stop haunting me as you do?'

'Oh, Rose, do you not see it is you that haunts me. Beneath that beautiful veneer lies something wicked indeed.' He pulled abruptly away, as if agitated by his own words.

'You mock me.'

'No, Rose, I do not.' Letting out a long sigh, he continued. 'Come, let us go inside, it will be time to eat soon.' Leaving my side, he walked towards the house and disappeared inside.

Hesitantly I followed, his words lingering in the cold evening air. How could I possibly haunt him? After all, I was just a girl.

CHAPTER 12

Daylight was fading outside and the dining room was bathed in the vibrant glow of candlelight. I sat myself across from Mother and forced a smile. She looked tired, worn. How long ago had her hair begun to grey?

Mr Weir had not yet joined us. I was hopeful he would not come at all.

'How are you finding things, Kirstin? Are you adjusting well enough?' Mother asked.

'I am adjusting well enough indeed. There is nothing left for me to do really. I even managed to take some time to sit in the garden and begin a new book.'

'How lovely. See the change is doing you a world of good already. I knew it would,' she said, smiling.

Although the words I spoke were true, I still felt as though I was deceiving her and it pained me to do so. I could feel the words rising in my throat, I needed to warn her.

Mr Weir entered the room. I choked my words back down, pushing them deep within my belly. 'I am glad to see everyone is making themselves at home. Sarah, you are simply the picture of perfection. Wherever did you find that dress you are wearing?'

Mr Weir slithered across the room and placed a kiss on Mother's hand.

He took his place at the end of the table. Mother was seated to his right and I to his left. 'Where is the cook with our food? I am absolutely ravenous!'

The three of us glanced uncomfortably around the table at one another. This was the first time that we had been in the same room together since Mr Weir had first come to our lodgings.

Mother shifted uncomfortably in her seat. 'Shall I go and check on the food?'

'Thank you, Sarah, but there is really no need. I am sure it will arrive in due course.' He smiled falsely. 'I trust you are both settling in all right. If there is anything further you require, please let me know and I shall see to it that it is provided for you.'

'That is most kind, Mr Weir, but you have done so much for us as it is. Wouldn't you agree, Kirstin?' Mother asked.

'Yes, we do not wish to impose too greatly,' I responded, trying my best to sound sincere.

'Nonsense, what is mine is yours. I have been on my own for so long that it is simply nice to have others to share this house with.'

Chapman entered the room with our food, bringing to an end the insufferable pleasantries.

Not raising my eyes from my plate I ate mechanically and in silence.

Mother ate, laughed and acted as any woman would in the company of a man she had taken a fancy to. Yet she never forgot her place. She remained the faithful servant, never overstepping her bounds. That was her weakness. She allowed herself to be bound by the limitations of her position.

I presume that Mr Weir saw this too, for his interest in her seemed to dim like the candles that surrounded us.

Our meal finally came to an end and I chose to excuse myself to avoid the risk of being left alone with Mr Weir.

I escaped into the dark hallway. I could hear the faint murmurs of Chapman and the cook and hoped that the shadows would conceal me; I did not wish to speak with anyone. Once safely past the kitchen, I leaned against the wall and exhaled while slowly lowering myself to the floor.

'I thought perhaps you might be here, lurking in the shadows,' Mr Weir said quietly, appearing from around the corner. 'You were so quiet at dinner I thought that I would do best to come check on you.' He crouched down in front of me and lifted my chin with his hand.

I looked up at him. 'I am tired, Oliver, and wish to be left alone. Please understand that I am only here for her, because it is what she wanted. Can't you see she wants nothing more than to please you?'

'To me she is nothing more than my employee. Why pretend there is something more when there is not? I admit I find her devotion charming, but to say that means I must care for her would be absurd.' He spoke quietly, just above a whisper so as not to be overheard.

Pulling my chin down to my knees I felt comfort in their support. 'She may be naive but she is still my mother. I can't let you hurt her. I won't!' I rose to my feet and looked down at him. How small he could look at times.

As I pushed by him and re-entered the dining room, he did not follow. Bidding Mother goodnight, I kissed her on the forehead and headed upstairs. Mr Weir had not moved. He sat crouched in the shadows.

The night was still young but I did not feel like socialising any longer. Entering my bedroom I closed the door behind me.

Pouring some water from a pitcher into a porcelain basin I washed myself as best I could before changing into a clean nightshift.

A short while later I was sitting at the dressing table brushing out my hair when I heard the muffled sound of voices coming from the hallway. Standing, I moved quietly to the door and listened. It was Mother and Mr Weir.

I opened the door slightly, just enough to see out and tried to hear what they were speaking of.

The two of them were standing in front of her chamber door. He was saying something about my father and how difficult it must have been for her to raise me all on her own.

Each word he spoke was meticulously chosen; he was spoon-feeding her lies and hungrily Mother swallowed each and every word.

As angry as I was there was nothing I could do to intervene. She was responsible for her own choices and I had to respect them no matter how naive they were.

Closing the door I walked over to the bed and climbed under the heavy mass of covers. As my eyes gave heed to the darkness, the dream came to me once more.

The mysterious forest surrounded me once again. I could see my father in the distance. He was kneeling before the pond, weeping, 'Why will you not come to me, Rose… Your destiny lies here.' As he said this he motioned towards the shimmering body of water, which is more luminous than ever. As he turned towards me, I could see the tears wet upon his face, but as I reached for him he vanished.

CHAPTER 13

As I returned to consciousness, I sensed I was no longer alone. My vision was still blurred from sleep but the candle at my bedside had been lit and I could see the outline of a figure kneeling beside me. As the stench of liquor overpowered my senses, I knew at once that it was Mr Weir.

I did not have the energy to act surprised; after all, this had not been the first time I had woken to find him watching me sleep.

'Get out,' was all I managed to say before rolling over, and pretending to return to sleep.

The bed shifted as he sat beside me. His breath grew hot upon my neck. My heart raced.

'Why do you refuse me so? Am I so repulsive to you?' he asked, pressing his face into my hair. I could feel the wetness of his tears on my neck. 'I should have never agreed to hire your mother. I should have known by the way your father spoke of you that I would not be able to resist falling in love with you.'

Had I misheard? 'When did you speak with my father?' I asked, turning quickly to face him.

'What does it matter now? He is dead, and you are here.' He reached out and, grasping my face within his hands, lowered his brow to rest gently against mine.

'It matters – of course, it matters. You knew my father?' I asked, trying to peel his hands from my face; they would not budge.

'Oh Rose... we had the same occupation. Did it never occur to you that we might have crossed paths at some point?' He lifted his eyes to mine. The tears now gone.

'But it was Prudence, your maid, who recommended Mother. That is why you hired her. That is why we are here.' As I spoke the words I knew that I had always somehow known that was not the full truth. I had wanted to believe in the coincidence, in the fragment of hope that this had not all been planned from the beginning.

'Do you really think it is all a coincidence that you and I have found one another? Rose, I sought Prudence out to come work for me. I wanted to learn more about you and your mother. I was curious. I found myself obsessed with the family of another man while my own was falling apart. I didn't understand why... not until I saw you for the first time. Then I knew. I knew we were meant to be together. That there had been a reason for it all.'

He wrapped his arms tightly around me. I tried to push him away but he had sobered up a little and was too strong to fight off.

'Why will you not have me, Rose? I am yours – all I want is you!' He pressed his lips hard against mine. I bit down drawing blood. My cheek stung as he hit me with the back of his hand.

'I hate you! You ask for my love, but your own heart is incapable of truly loving,' I cried, scrambling to get off the bed. My hands grabbed at the bedding in fistfuls as I tried to propel myself forward. But it was of no use.

Mr Weir grabbed me by the hair and tugged me backwards into his embrace. 'Rose, please calm yourself!' His arms were tight around mine, binding me to him.

I closed my eyes tight, trying to escape the reality of the moment. What could I have done to prevent this? How could it all have been avoided? He had crept into my life like a weed, and now he was taking over, killing off all that was pure inside me. Why had I not just confided in Mother? Perhaps she would have listened. After all, there must be some motherly care left in her; she was not so smitten, surely!

He spun me around to face him then pinned me to the bed

underneath his weight. I closed my eyes and prayed silently for God to intervene – to take pity on His child.

'Stay still, my love… I won't hit you again, I promise. But you must be still.' Mr Weir's hands moved away from my arms and grabbed my face. 'Look at me,' he ordered and I obeyed.

He kissed my cheek, softly moving his moist lips slowly down to my neck. 'Oh, Rose, I have wanted you like this for so long.'

Tears streamed from my eyes. I tried to focus on anything but him – anything but the awareness of him pressing hard against me.

He was now kissing my collarbone, pulling down at the fabric of my nightshift to clear the path for his lips. Pressing against me he groaned, cupping his hand around one of my breasts. His breath was moist and hot upon my skin.

'Oliver, stop please, I beg of you,' I sobbed, making one last plea to reason with him.

'Shh… It's all right, Rose.' His mouth pressed against mine as he worked his hand down across the delicate curves of my body. I felt the cool air on my thighs as he slowly lifted my nightshift. 'Don't be afraid.'

But I was afraid; afraid of what would happen if I tried to stop him and equally afraid of what was about to happen if I did not.

'Look at me, Rose.' He looked down at me with his dark ebony eyes as he caressed me, invading me with his hand.

I closed my eyes, wincing at the sudden unexpected discomfort.

'Open your eyes, Rose. I want to see you.' He would not even allow me to escape into the comfort of my own thoughts while he robbed me of my virtue.

He began to unfasten his trousers and I knew what was about to happen. I felt his weight on top of me, readying himself. Silently I prayed for it to be quickly over with.

'What is the meaning of this?' An alarmed voice suddenly called from the doorway.

'Mother?' Although my eyes were wet with tears, I thought I

saw her standing before us. 'Is it really you? Why do you just stand there? Will you not help me?'

She stood frozen, too consumed by her own heartache to come to my aid.

Mr Weir turned to face her. 'It is not what it seems, Sarah. She was having a bad dream. I only meant to calm her.'

I took advantage quickly of his distraction and struggled free from his clutches. I dragged myself backwards – grasping for air, clenching the freedom, the space. I leapt off the bed towards the door.

I could feel him close behind me, trying to stop me leaving. Mother sat there crouched in the doorway, the light barely illuminating her tears; I stumbled past her into the hallway. I could hear Chapman calling out from the bottom of the stairs – footsteps racing heavily behind me, stomping, pounding.

Downwards I flew, my feet hitting the stairs hard. I was moving too fast. My head struck against the handrail.

When I opened my eyes, Chapman was standing over me, a look of great concern upon his face.

'Rose, are you all right? What in heavens is going on up there?'

Somehow I gained the strength to rise, to open the front door and to keep running. I did not glance back to see if he followed. But even out in the streets I could feel his presence. Mr Weir would always be watching, waiting for me to return.

CHAPTER 14

I could no longer see the glow of the city behind me. My legs were heavy and sore but I forced myself to keep going, to put as much distance between Mr Weir and me as possible.

The night was dark and cool but the brilliance of the moonlight guided my way. I soon crossed the treeline of a forest. Where was I? It was as though the deep woods had appeared from out of nowhere.

I ran deeper and deeper into the shelter of the trees, more frightened by what followed behind me than the darkness ahead. When I no longer felt as though I was being pursued, I allowed myself to stop running. I sank to my knees, gasping for breath, tears trickling slowly into my mouth.

I am not sure how long I sat there weeping. When my tears finally came to an end, I took notice of the strange silence. There was no bustling of leaves, no swaying of branches, no owls hooting, nor critters scurrying – just silence.

I lifted my face from my hands and scanned the moonlit trees – in the distance shone a light so bright it was as if a star had fallen from the heavens. I rose to my feet and walked towards it.

Was I dreaming?

The source of light grew larger as I approached. It seemed to shimmer under the glow of the moon. When I finally drew near enough I could clearly see it was a small body of water.

I knelt and looked down at my reflection. My face was red and swollen where Mr Weir had hit me and I had scrapes along my arms and legs. I was filthy.

I stepped into the water. The sensation was cooling on my

sore raw feet. I took a step forward, and then another until I was submerged in the water.

I felt cleansed as if the water was washing away the memory of Mr Weir's touch.

I did not know where I would go from here but I knew I could never return to that house. I knew that, if I did return, it would be only a matter of time before he finished what he had begun.

I closed my eyes, lifted my legs and leaned back, letting myself float on the water's surface. Then, through the muffled veil of water, I thought I could hear someone calling out to me, calling my name.

I lifted my head and quickly looked around me. No one was there. I swam a bit closer to the edge; it was shallow enough now to stand. Mud squished up between my toes.

'Is someone there?' I called out.

I heard it again. This time more clearly. 'Rose,' the voice whispered, long and slow.

'Who's there? Show yourself!' I called out again, still unable to make out anyone else beyond the circle of trees.

The voice continued. It was now as though it was calling from all directions. I could not make out if it was male or female. I was frightened.

And then in a flash I saw her – so young, so beautiful. Her skin was as pale as the moonlight yet her hair was as dark as night.

'Rose,' she uttered one last time before capturing me in her embrace. She moved so quickly I had not even time to react. I felt a sharp pain as she tore into my neck with her teeth. I reached up trying to pry her off of me and felt my father's ring slip from my finger and down into the water below.

She drained the blood from me, the sensation unlike anything I had ever experienced before. And as the blood streamed down over my alabaster skin the water around me turned to crimson. I felt weak and, as she detached herself from me, my legs gave way beneath me and I slowly began to sink down into the water.

I felt cold. I could feel the water no longer. Something warm was dripping into my mouth. It tasted metallic. My lips found the source of the liquid and I latched on, pulling the open wound of her wrist down towards me; the flow increased.

I stared into her glistening amber eyes; they seemed to smile at me. I felt calm. She stroked my hair and leaned forward, kissing my forehead. Then she was gone.

I lay on the forest floor staring up at the twinkling sky above me. I could feel my heart beginning to slow and the rising of my chest becoming less frequent as I struggled with my last breath.

The pain was agonising and I needed relief. Then it came. Limb by limb, my body began to numb. The darkness came over me like a wave and I slipped gratefully into the nothingness that is death.

CHAPTER 15

My eyes flickered open to the brilliant glow of the moonlight. How long had I been gone? Days perhaps?

The forest was no longer silent. A cacophony of sounds surrounded me, overwhelming my senses. I could see everything. My eyes shifted focus from one object to the next at rapid speed. I screwed my eyes tight and inhaled. The pain was gone, but so was the usual feeling of relief such would normally bring. No heart contracted in reaction to the influx of breath; I felt no need to exhale.

Crawling over to the water, I examined my reflection. Glaring back at me were a set of glowing emerald eyes, my eyes. My hair was transformed into a copper mass of perfectly spun curls, as if angels had weaved each lock from the rays of the breaking dawn.

I reached towards the water; my pale white skin was splattered with blood. Her blood. I splashed some water on my face, the diluted red liquid dripped down my hands. What had I become?

I needed to get out of there. I feared she would return. Rising I began making my way home. I was no longer lost. London was calling me back, her glowing lamplight guiding me through the darkness.

CHAPTER 16

Here I was standing in front of Mr Weir's house staring up at the amber glow of his window. Why was I here? I could feel the hatred building within me. I needed answers.

The door was unlocked. Quietly I ascended the stairs. The glow of a fire radiated from beneath Mr Weir's bedroom door. I placed my fingers around the brass doorknob and turned.

Mr Weir sat asleep in front of the fire, a bottle of whisky clutched within his hand. I crept towards him. My shadow cast upon the wall by the light of the fire seemed enormous. I was reminded of my newfound strength. Kneeling in front of him, I placed my face against his forehead and whispered, 'Oliver, wake up.'

His eyes opened wide. For a brief moment, his face held a look of amazement and fear at the sight of me.

'Rose, thank God you're back. Sarah… your mother … has been out looking for you every day since you left. Where have you been?'

'It matters not,' I snapped, trying to resist my urge to kill him before I had my questions finally answered. 'Oliver, I have to ask you something and I want the absolute truth – no more lies. Were you there the night my father died?'

'Why are you asking me this? What does it matter now?' he said, turning his face away from mine.

'Because I need to hear you say it. Were you there?' I asked again, as calmly as I could manage.

'Yes, I was there. Is that what you want to hear?' he shouted.

'I want the truth. You have been lying to me since the day we met and I need to know what happened to my father.'

'Where have you been, Rose?' he asked, his eyes now studying mine. 'You look different somehow.'

'Answer me!' I shouted, grabbing his face in my hands. 'What happened the night my father died?'

He looked at me in fear. 'Rose, I played no part in your father's death. That is the truth.'

'Liar!' I was overcome with rage, with loss. Tears began to flow from my eyes. I lowered my head to his forehead and placed my lips firmly upon his. I could taste the metallic wetness of my tears as they passed between our lips.

Until that moment I had been unaware of the full result of my transformation, but as I felt my teeth sharpen beneath my lips I began to realise what I had become.

I swiftly moved my lips to his neck and began to draw the hot red liquid from his veins. He gasped and then with the faintest of words he spoke: 'It was her...' Clutching my hand tightly, he pressed something into my hand. It was a piece of paper, a letter, heavily worn as if it had been read a thousand times.

'What is this?' I asked, examining it further. I inhaled sharply as I realised what it was – a letter from myself to my father, sent to him on his last trip before he died. The pages were damp and spattered with blood, fresh upon old.

'I didn't mean to take it.' He pressed his lips to my ear. 'I was scared. You have to believe me, Rose. It was not me... I saw her, that thing.'

'What are you talking about – you saw whom?'

'...I thought he was good as dead.' Mr Weir's face contorted in pain as his body convulsed, the ripple of impending death surging through him limb by limb. 'If I had of known he would live, I would have hel...helped him,' he said, drawing in a desperate breath of air. 'Forgive me.'

But I could not. After everything he had done how could I ever forgive him?

The fire flickered before me. I felt comforted and warm. The sweet and sticky elixir of life flooded into me from the open wounds on his neck. I could hear as his heartbeat began to slow, the hypnotic rhythm lulling me to sleep as I curled myself into his lap. Wasn't this what he had wanted?

I had nearly drifted off, my fangs now retracted, my milky white flesh flushed and rosy from the intake of blood, when I heard the faint creak of a floorboard in the hallway.

Faster than human eyes could trace, I was standing at the doorway of Mr Weir's room, my hand firmly wrapped around my mother's neck. I could feel the movement in her throat as she tried to swallow, stifling a scream. Her panicked eyes were searching mine, trying to find evidence of what was once her daughter beneath the blood-stained face of the girl before her.

'How long have you been here?' I questioned her.

'Long enough, Kirstin,' she managed to say as I loosened my grip around her neck.

'Come. Sit,' I instructed, releasing her from my grasp and motioning towards Mr Weir's bed.

She did as I bid her, cautiously stepping across the threshold into the bedroom towards the bed, her eyes fixed on Mr Weir's lifeless body while she did so.

'Well, well, Mother, what am I going to do with you?'

I was now standing in front of her, or rather over her. She seemed so small and fragile before me. I could hear her heart beating rapidly. Her breath fast and eager. I could even smell the perspiration rising from the flesh of her palms.

'My darling daughter, my lovely Rose, I plead of you, have pity on me. Have I not cared for you? Are you not still my child whom I brought forth into this world?' Her arms were outstretched, palms facing up as so many humans do.

'It is true, Mother: you did push me forth from your womb into this dark and dreary world. But it was Father who cared for me; it was he who provided for me. And what became of me after he passed away? Who took care of me then? Who protected me from her dear master?' With these words I lifted Mother from the bed and sat her down beside Mr Weir's motionless body.

I knelt before her and gazed deep into her eyes. They were wide and moist with tears. But they were not tears of redemption, nor tears of a mother's sorrow; they were tears of weakness and of fear. In that moment I took pity on her.

In her tears I had seen her truth, finally understood that she was a weak-willed woman who never had enough sense to look out for anyone but herself. She had never rose above her very nature as a woman of those times. She knew nothing else than servitude towards men.

I took my mother's face in my hands and locked my eyes on hers. 'Listen to my words, Mother. Your daughter is dead. One day I may come for you, but until that day you will forget me. You will forget what you have witnessed this evening. You will leave this place and never return.'

She rose and exited the room without saying a word. When I heard the front door close behind her I went to the window. I watched as she reached the end of the front path and stepped out into the opaque fog, disappearing into the darkness.

I turned and looked back at Mr Weir sitting lifeless in front of the dying flames. Unexpectedly, from deep inside me I felt a pang – a pang of remorse. I was now truly alone in this world.

Moving away from the window, I climbed back into Mr Weir's lap and placed his arm around my waist. The fire was now a glow of grey and orange embers. I began to weep. The tears that trickled down my face were not salt water but gentle streams of blood. I had been crying blood.

Leaning over him I planted a firm kiss upon his lips, bidding a final farewell.

Then, lifting my defeated body from his lap, I walked towards the door and said goodbye to my mortal life and goodbye to my innocence.

PART II

From the ashes she will be born anew,
Like a bright and beautiful peacock, she will rise,
And tempt you with her brilliant plume.

CHAPTER 1

For the first time in as long as I could remember I did not feel sad, or afraid, or worried. I felt free.

I answered to no one. My life was my own, or so I thought. But I was not really alive, not any longer. There was no heartbeat within the walls of my chest. I had no need to breathe; if I became injured, I healed almost instantly.

However, I was quickly discovering the limitations of my newfound condition. Within me was an unquenchable hunger I could not satisfy. Food did not agree with me and would come immediately back up. Drink I could tolerate. I had heard tales of creatures who fed off the blood of the living – vampires. Was this what I had become? I had fed on Mr Weir, had I not? Was it not good? Did I not feel all the better for it – revitalised?

When the sun began to rise on the second day of my rebirth I retreated into the depths of the underground, seeking shelter within the railway tunnels. I was not certain what would become of me if I stayed above ground but I felt a pull from deep within me to be away from the light, to scurry into the shadows of darkness.

It was there that I found sleep, deep within the veins of the city that flowed with life as London awoke. The hum soothed me.

The setting of the sun roused me, as if my body knew it was safe to emerge. I could hear life active all around me – I could smell their sweet elixir. A hunger stirred within me.

I surfaced from the depths of London in a frenzy of need. My first unfortunate victim that evening was a busker whose playful melody had gained my attention. I dragged him into an alleyway and hastily drained him. Almost instantly I felt more at ease, but not yet satisfied.

I was more strategic in choosing my next victim. I was filthy and covered in the dry crimson offerings of my previous victims.

She caught my attention the instant she came into my view. Young and sweet-looking, a refined lady of no more than eighteen. Her hair was a golden mass of angelic curls, her skin milky white. She was slender and thin about the waist, her bosom slight and youthful. Upon her head she wore the most wonderful hat that matched the colour and fabric of her plum-coloured dress.

She did not see me approach her and was startled when I suddenly appeared before her. Our eyes met and she looked upon me with a gentle softness. 'You gave me a fright, Miss,' she said before examining me further. 'You are injured. I shall call for help.'

'No. Do not call out,' I said to her, not moving my eyes from hers. She obeyed as if compelled to do so.

I took her hand and led her towards a place where the lamplight did not shine. We were now safely concealed by the darkness.

'I am in need of your dress. You will give it to me.' I spoke to her in the same fashion as before.

'Of course!' She nodded as she began to unfasten the buttons of her dress.

I watched as she peeled away each of the layers, placing them into my outstretched arms as she did so. She now stood before me nude. The soft moonlight illuminated the pale curves of her form, the hunger building again inside of me.

I placed her clothing gently in a pile beside me and stepped towards her. My teeth sharpened. She took in a sharp breath and moved away from me.

In my new form my body moved quite easily, and at great speed. I held her in my arms and looked down upon her. 'Shh… Do not be afraid,' I comforted her. I then lowered my mouth to her delicate neck and tore into her flesh.

Her blood spilled forth into my mouth and I drank greedily.

Her heart beat quickly at first but then began to slow. When it became as faint as a whisper I stopped; her body fell to my feet as I released her. She would live.

The hour was drawing late and the activity of the streets thinned as people retreated into their homes. I made my way down to the Embankment with my bundle of acquired clothing and located a secluded area in which to bathe.

The dark waters of the Thames were cool and unpleasant. But they served their purpose. The foul-smelling water washed the layers of blood and filth that had accumulated over the past few days. When I was dressed I could once again pass as human.

I wandered the streets of London that evening as if under a spell, my senses overwhelmed. Everything appeared so vibrant and full of life. The sounds of the city were amplified tenfold.

CHAPTER 2

Each night I emerged from my shelter beneath the city to hunt. I sought out the wicked and vile vermin that ran rampant in the streets of the East End. They were like a plague that needed to be eradicated.

The more I fed, the better I became at the hunt. At first the speed at which I now moved proved challenging to conceal and great concentration was required to manipulate my limbs into a slower, more human-like manner. My smooth white skin was so thin, almost transparent, and each time I fed my veins would become engorged, turning from grey to bright crimson. In time, I learned to keep my limbs covered and took to wearing a cloak even though I never grew cold.

To the unstudied eye I still appeared to be a young lady and no one suspected that underneath the pretty veneer lay such a fiend. But I could not survive underground forever, feeding off the weak and forgotten. It was too tragic, too inhuman to live in that way. I was beginning to lose myself, to become no better than the vile loathsome people I hunted. So I made a choice. I would take back that life which was stolen from me all those years ago.

Thus began my life of theft and deceit. I stole not only the lives of my victims but also whatever was in their purses.

Over time I slowly built up a small fortune, but I found I could not easily spend it. For one, most shops were not open during the evening; secondly, owing to my age and gender, I was limited in what I could actually purchase. For instance, I could not purchase property, I could not manage my own affairs or open a bank account. I resorted to storing my wealth in one of the unused and forgotten underground tunnels.

I was again growing tired of this new way of living. I was no better off than I had been whilst residing with Mr Weir. It was then that I thought of a way to improve things. As ashamed as I was to admit it, the most valuable asset I had in my possession was the bewitching effect I had upon men and I resolved to begin using this to my advantage.

I sought out gentlemen who were willing to provide me with lodgings and to perform those tasks that I was unable to do myself during the day. And while some expected payment in kind, others simply enjoyed my company. Needless to say, the former met swift and untimely deaths, while the latter could be allowed to live until I grew tired of them and moved on.

The irony of my new way of life was not lost on me. I suppose if you fight against something for long enough you eventually give in. But I convinced myself that things were different then they had been with Mr Weir. For one, I was in control now; there were no games, no manipulation; there was only my needs and wants and what I was prepared to do to fulfil them.

I could hardly blame these men for desiring me; I had become irresistible in my new form. I suppose that was part of the package; you can't very well be a savage sucker of blood and stealer of lives if you look like you have just crawled out of the depths of hell.

Life was good. In a way, I felt as though this is what my life might have been like had Father still been alive – minus the company of multiple male companions… and the killings. But I would have been out in society, sought after by men and lavished with gifts as they vied to win my affections.

And so this is what the first six months of my new life entailed: a seamless rhythm that satisfied all my needs – or so I thought. Such is the naive mentality of any sixteen-year-old girl. I thought very much as a child still, despite all I had done and all I had witnessed. It was not until I met Henry that I became a woman; that I finally understood what it is to want for nothing and to feel cherished.

CHAPTER 3

It was a balmy evening in spring when I stepped across the threshold into a grand white terraced house in Mayfair. I decorated the arm of my most recent companion, Mr Deighton, who had been invited to a private ball. The host, I had been told, was an important member of society, the son of a duke.

London had come alive during the Season and there never seemed a lack of entertaining things to occupy one's time in the evenings.

Everyone ate and drank and danced, gluttonously devouring the richness on offer. I was enamoured by the spectacle and sat quietly by while my escort engaged in conversation with two gentlemen next to me. My eyes wandered over the room, out of habit scanning the sea of pastel chiffon and black silk for potential donors. My stomach tightened and I inhaled sharply to stifle the pain. I was hungry.

Through the clamour of the swaying crowd, I became aware of someone watching me and, as I turned my gaze to locate my admirer, my eyes locked with his across the room.

My eyes quickly evaluated him in fragments, taking in each delightful detail, one by one. His soft yet wild golden locks, his lean yet strong figure, his pale smooth skin dotted with brown freckles.

I looked away quickly, then feeling somewhat recovered from my initial appraisal, I returned my gaze to his direction. To my delight and surprise he still looked upon me with his glistening aquamarine eyes. Impossibly, I felt my dead heart flutter, as one might feel the movement of a limb after it had been lost.

I was suddenly aware that I was sitting too still. A human woman would fidget, play with her hair or wave her fan. I retrieved my recently acquired fan from my lap. I quickly opened and closed it.

The golden-haired man's eyes widened. He smiled and this had the most wonderful effect on his features. I had never seen anyone so handsome. But my admiration of him stirred the darkness within me and I felt my teeth sharpen beneath my soft pink lips. I turned quickly away.

I needed a moment to collect myself, to regain my composure. I excused myself to my companion. He, barely breaking away from his conversation, waved his hand in agreement. I was relieved that his lack of manners prevented him from insisting on escorting me and in a moment I was out in the safety of the foyer.

I entered the dressing room, which thankfully was unoccupied. I felt comforted by the momentary solitude. I sat before the gleaming mirror and assessed myself. My eyes were a vibrant shade of chartreuse and the sharp tips of two white canines peaked out from beneath my rose-coloured lips. I closed my eyes and sat silently in meditation. I needed to stifle my need before I could go back into the ballroom.

When I once again felt collected, I rose, smoothing the invisible creases of my lilac dress, and returned to the ballroom.

My escort hurried over to me and took my arm. 'You keep them waiting, Rose,' he said. 'Our host has enquired after you and has requested your next dance be his.'

I was curious as to why I was on the receiving end of such an honour. 'As I am not otherwise engaged I see no reason to object.'

'Certainly... Ah, he approaches now.'

My golden-haired admirer glided towards us. He was our host?

'Miss Rose, may I introduce our host, Lord Henry.' My companion had answered my silent question.

I greeted our host with a bow, as was the custom.

'It is a pleasure to make your acquaintance,' Lord Henry said. 'Shall I have the pleasure of dancing with you?' His voice was smooth and refined.

I lifted my head ever so slightly and met his eyes. 'With pleasure, Sir,' I responded somewhat apprehensively.

He invited my arm to rest in the crook of his and we joined the other dancing partners. 'I have not seen you before. Are you recently out in society?'

'Yes. This is my first Season, and my first private ball.'

'I hope you have found it to your satisfaction?' he queried, with a look of reproachful self-doubt.

'Oh yes – very much so,' I reassured him, even though I had not received as many introductions and dances as I would have liked.

'You and your gentleman – how are you two acquainted? I have asked round and no one seems to know anything about you, yet they know of your Mr Deighton.'

'Mr Deighton is my uncle. He has been kind enough to offer me residence in London for the Season.' I knew that Mr Deighton had a number of brothers and sisters and we had rehearsed this lie for our public engagements.

My response seemed to satisfy his curiosity. 'I have been watching you, Miss Rose. I find you most intriguing.' As he spun me round to face him, I saw that he wore an expression of great seriousness.

'You flatter me, Sir. No doubt there are many ladies in our company this evening who are more worthy of your affections than I.' I spoke quietly as not to draw the attention of those dancing near by.

'For one so beautiful you are too modest,' he reproached me. 'I find that most refreshing.'

'I fear I am not the enigma you make me out to be. Are not all women a mystery until discovered by a man?'

'In a way I suppose you are quite right. Nevertheless you have sparked a curiosity in me.'

The music had come to a halt and our dance was over.

We bowed and he took my arm leading me in the direction of my escort. 'Will you be at your uncle's all through the Season? I would very much like to call on you,' he inquired urgently just as we were about to part ways.

'No, you mustn't call on me,' I whispered, unwrapping my arm from around his.

'Please – I must see you again. I will write to you, just give me your address,' he pleaded.

'Do not ask this of me.' I did desire to look upon him again, to be near to him. But I knew doing so could bring no good to either of us.

I turned to my escort, who had drawn near. 'Mr Deighton, I have grown tired of dancing. If it pleases you, I should like to be taken home now.'

'Certainly, Rose, I shall escort you to the dressing room to gather your things and I will call for the carriage.' He turned to our host before departing. 'Lord Henry, thank you for a most enjoyable evening.'

'The enjoyment was mine.' Lord Henry took my hand in his, lifting it to his full pink lips. 'Goodnight, Rose.'

By the time Mr Deighton and I had returned to his residence I was ravenous. I locked myself in my temporary chambers, requesting not to be disturbed, fearful of what I might do. The excitement of the evening had aroused such a hunger in me it was beyond suppression. I could not stop thinking about Lord Henry. His scent lingered about me; it was intoxicating.

I sealed myself in that room for three days. On the evening of the third day I emerged, having managed to push my need so deep within me that I felt able to interact with others once more.

CHAPTER 4

One cannot hope to stay lost forever and the evening I rose again was the day on which Lord Henry finally found me.

'You have received a letter, Rose, from Lord Henry,' Mr Deighton announced as I joined him in the dining room.

'Oh? I wonder what it says. I cannot think why someone of his high standing would have reason to write to me.'

'The letter is on my desk in the study. I was instructed to make sure that you opened it straightaway but did not want to disturb you while you have been so unwell.' Mr Deighton explained. He really was a genuinely kind man. I was lucky to have made his acquaintance. He had found me wandering the streets one evening and offered me a bed and a warm meal. So far he had expected nothing in return for his hospitality, and as far as I could tell he simply enjoyed having me around.

'Thank you, Sir. I think I shall go fetch the letter in case it is a matter of urgency.'

'Will you not eat?'

'I have not yet regained my appetite. Perhaps I will have the cook prepare me some broth in a short while.'

'Very well. If I cannot persuade you otherwise, you may be excused.'

I lit a small lamp in Mr Deighton's study and located the letter. 'Dear Miss Rose' was scrawled on the outside of the crisp white paper. I broke the wax seal and read its contents.

My Enigma,

Despite your protest, I am writing in the hope that I may see you again. I pray that this letter finds you, and that you have not already departed from your uncle's by the time you receive this correspondence.

I have thought of you day and night since we parted. Have you thought of me?

My comrades have commented that I seem distracted and melancholy. If they only knew the torment I feel in longing for your company, they would understand the nature of my condition.

You insisted that I must not call on you. I do not know what is behind this cruel request, but I shall obey. Perhaps you would come to me? I shall be in this evening and it would give me cause for great jubilation should you call.

Affectionately yours,

Henry.

What was I to do? I wanted to see him more than I had wanted anything in a very long time, but I feared that I could not keep control of myself in his presence. No, I could not go to him.

I retreated back into my chambers, telling one of the maids that I was feeling unwell again and to let Mr Deighton know that I did not wish to be disturbed.

I lay on my bed and stared up at the ceiling. How long could I go without blood? I wondered. I had already begun to notice my senses becoming less sharp, my movement slowing.

Unable to bear the agony of my hunger any longer, I decided I needed to feed. I pulled on a cloak and a pair of boots and lifted the window sash. I might have weakened but I could still manage the two-storey drop down to the street.

I made my way through the darkened streets of London in search of a meal. Perhaps you know that feeling when you are so far beyond hunger that no ordinary morsel will do, when your desire has grown to such a state that you crave a taste so satisfying that it will trump all other meals? This is what I felt; this is what drove me back towards that white terraced house in Mayfair.

I rapped on the glossy black door that stood tall in front of me. A finely dressed man soon answered.

'I am Miss Rose to see Lord Henry,' I said and then added, 'he has asked me to call.'

He opened the door and ushered me in, taking my cloak and hat. 'This way, Miss. He has retired to his private quarters on the second floor.'

My hunger built as we ascended the stairs to the second floor. I should not have come and thought immediately of turning and leaving. Inexplicably, I felt compelled to continue onwards.

As we entered the room Henry rose to greet me. 'I did not think you would come.' We were now alone in the privacy of his private sitting room.

'It was not my intention. I was out walking and found myself at your door.'

'Well, then, I am overjoyed by this serendipity. Please sit.'

I took a seat on the nearby settee. He placed a book he had been reading face down on top of a small rectangular table and sat down next to me. He was strangely free in his actions, as if he was answerable to no one.

'Would you like a drink?'

'No, thank you.'

'But you don't mind if I do?' he asked.

I nodded my approval, and he rose and gracefully made his way over to a small drinks cabinet. Removing the stopper from a crystal decanter, he poured an amber-coloured liquid into a glass and returned to his place beside me.

His proximity to me was becoming unbearable and I was growing concerned, not for myself, but for his safety, as I was ravenous and his scent was so alluring.

'Do you always abstain from drink?' he inquired. The glow of the fire reflected in his eyes like little flames dancing upon the sea. I longed to bathe in them.

'Yes, I suppose I do. I would argue that drinking is a man's vice, not a lady's.'

'I suppose you are quite right. Although would you agree that women are not without vices?'

'Indeed, I would agree such is very true. Women often behave very foolishly and are not as virtuous as men often believe us to be. That is a false notion embedded in our minds by modern society.'

Henry laughed. 'You amuse me, Rose. I find your views most invigorating.'

'Please, Sir, you flatter me too much. I only speak what I think to be true.'

He took a swig of his drink and placed the heavy glass down on the table. 'You are very beautiful, Rose. I feel quite unhinged in your presence.'

'Lord Henry, please, you must not speak this way.'

'You find me improper?'

'It is not that; it is only that your words stir something within me. I do not trust myself when I am with you.'

'Do you wish to leave? Just say the words and I'll take you home.' He placed his hand on top of mine.

'No, I do not wish to leave.' I lowered my head, ashamed of my reciprocated desire.

He lifted my chin so that my gaze met his. 'I am pleased to hear you say that. To part ways with you so soon would cause me great disappointment.' He leaned forward and brushed his warm lips across my cool cheek. His warmth radiated down through my body igniting the dormant embers deep within.

His lips were soft and gentle as they grazed my skin. My lips sought out his and received them eagerly. I wanted nothing more in that moment than to devour every inch of him. I pulled him savagely towards me. His eyes were wide with surprise at the swiftness and strength of my movement, but he did not pull away.

He smothered me with rapture-filled kisses, exploring my form with his eager hands. My petticoats and shift were soon taken up and my body responded instantly to his touch. A new hunger had risen inside me.

A current radiated through my body. I felt alive. As he unfastened his breeches I did not desire for one moment to stop him. He lowered himself on top of me and locked eyes with me before entering me. I could not help but cry out during those initial thrusts. I felt my teeth sharpen.

The discomfort soon gave way to pleasure of the most enjoyable kind. As our bodies contorted into one I could no longer control my hunger. I sunk my exposed fangs deep into his throat and drank. The blissful intake of his blood combined with the quickening of his rhythm sent me over the edge; I felt my body explode and tremble with release. Henry groaned loudly and collapsed on top of me shaking.

We lay there in silence. I felt the warmth of his blood streaming through me, thawing me from the inside out. My skin was slowly gaining a rosy hue.

After a moment Henry sat up and pulled me into his arms, kissing my forehead gently. 'Are you hurt? I fear I have caused you injury in my haste.'

'Do not fret – I will heal. Besides, it is I who should be asking after your injuries.' I examined his neck. I had only taken enough blood to quench my thirst, but not enough to weaken him greatly.

'I am well, my pet, but tell me, what are you?'

'I do not know, not really. The one who made me this way did not explain.'

'*Made* you?'

'She drained me of my blood – I died. But then, like Christ, I was reborn, resurrected from death.' I paused, assessing Henry's reaction. He seemed calm and receptive. 'I require blood to continue living. I cannot withstand the daylight, I heal with great speed and my senses are more acute than ever they were when I was alive.'

'You are a vampire? But such is a creature of myth and legend.'

'But here I am before you. I live and breathe yet my heart does not beat… Feel!' I took Henry's hand and placed it over my chest where my still heart lay.

He pulled away his hand. 'Fascinating!'

'You're not scared?' I asked.

'On the contrary, I find you the most captivating creature I have ever met.' He pulled me towards him once more and kissed me. 'I would like you to stay with me tonight, and for however long you wish. If you accept my offer, I will write to your uncle at once. We can send for your things tomorrow.'

'Oh Henry, that is very kind of you but I could not impose on you like that. Tonight has been unexpected and wonderful, but you will soon tire of me.'

'My darling, I could no sooner tire of you than I could tire of the need to breathe. I find your presence most necessary,' he proclaimed. His manner was sincere and honest, and gave me no reason to doubt his words.

'Very well then, I shall stay with you until you express a desire to send me away.'

He smiled at my response. As much as I believed his feelings were true I had spent a great deal of time lately in the presence of men and had noted that to them all things are eventually disposable.

'Good, I am pleased. Now I must leave you for a moment to tend to some things. The room next to this is my bedchamber. You're welcome to wait in there for me. I won't be long.'

Henry stood and straightened himself, combing his fingers through his wild golden locks. He bent down and pressed his lips to mine. I felt my skin flush at the sensation. I could smell the sweetness of his blood that stained the two small wounds on his neck. I bit my thumb, drawing blood and rubbed it over the two marks; they healed instantly.

Once Henry had left the room I made my way over to the adjacent bedroom. Henry's bedroom was, as expected, grand and luxurious and furnished to the highest standard. In the middle of the room was a large four-poster bed with white-and-gold damask curtains. I wanted to lie in it, to touch something that was intimately his.

I had no lady's-maid to dress me each day so I never wore complicated fashions or a corset. As a result undressing was an easy enough task.

Stripped down to only my under-shift I pulled back the coverings and buried myself beneath them. I had not felt so at ease since I was a child. I was not hungry, or scared, or lonely. I felt content and, in that moment, I wanted for nothing.

Closing my eyes I fell into a deep and dreamless slumber. I had not dreamed since that night in the forest, the night I was changed. I was not sure whether I would ever dream again. Did the soulless dream?

A shift in weight upon the bed woke me. It was Henry. I recognised his sweet intoxicating scent. I opened my eyes. The bed-curtains were drawn but even in the darkness I could sense it was close to dawn.

'You smell sweet,' I said, nuzzling my nose into his neck. I felt my two sharp teeth suddenly protrude and pushed myself away from him abruptly. The last thing I wanted in that moment was to harm him, and I wasn't sure if I was capable of controlling my dark hunger yet.

'Shh… do not recoil,' Henry whispered, taking my hands in his and pulling me once again close to him. 'My beautiful Rose, I know that your great enchanting beauty also has thorns. But I do not fear their prick.' I felt him grow against me, his warm hands working their way up my shift.

I rolled on top of him and lifted my shift up and over my head. My hair was momentarily taken captive by the fabric before bouncing back into place.

Henry watched my every movement, as if under my spell. I had never been looked upon naked before, like this, but I did not feel shy. He caressed my skin and I felt my insides warm in response. I leaned forward and kissed him, and as I did so I felt the familiar sting of him burying himself inside of me. We moved in a synchronised rhythm, bathing in each other's desire.

I relinquished control and let my body fall under the weight of him. His skin was warm and moist against mine. My urge to bite him was unbearable. I wanted nothing more in that moment than to sink my teeth into his flesh and drink from him. As if reading my thoughts, Henry exposed his neck to me.

I turned my head. 'I don't want to hurt you.'

He grabbed my face and made me look at him. His eyes were full of passion and intensity. 'I want you to bite me, Rose.'

His words excited and aroused me. I grabbed him by his hair and pulled, sinking my razor-sharp teeth into his throbbing neck. The blood flowed into my mouth and I lapped it up lustfully. In that moment I felt one with him, as if the two of us had become one entity, rocking together in the euphoria of our exchange. I found it very difficult to stop this time but somehow I found the strength. I retracted my fangs and lapped at the wound with my tongue.

Henry kissed me sweetly. 'I think I love you, Rose.' He now lay beside me. His arm wrapped tight around my waist so that we were interlocked like two pieces that fit together. 'I knew the moment I saw you that we belonged like this. Strange, isn't it?' He closed his eyes and let out a deep slow breath, succumbing to the arms of sleep.

CHAPTER 5

I woke as the remaining sliver of daylight slipped away beneath the darkened horizon. The bed was empty beside me. I pushed off the layers of coverings and pulled back the bed-curtain. The room was quiet and empty but I could sense movement elsewhere in the house.

Folded on the end of the bed was a crisp white nightshift. Henry must have come in and left it for me. I climbed out of the bed and put it on.

There was a knock at the door and a stream of light penetrated the darkness as it opened ever so slightly. From behind the door came a meek feminine voice:

'Miss? Miss Rose, are you awake? I have been instructed by Lord Henry to draw you a bath.'

I opened the door fully and she stumbled forward as if startled by the action.

'Very well, lead the way,' I instructed curtly. There was something in her fragility that made me uneasy.

She led me down the hallway to the bathroom. As we entered the scent of jasmine and lavender filled the air. In the centre of the room stood a white porcelain bath-tub with a wooden crate placed in front of it. I disrobed and used the crate to raise myself to a less awkward height to step into the tub.

The night was dark and the flicker of candlelight danced across the pink-and-gold-papered walls.

The girl, who could not have been older than thirteen or fourteen, brought over a sponge and dipped it into the water. When it was sufficiently drenched she lifted it over my shoulders and squeezed so that the soft warm water streamed down my back and over my chest. It was a lovely sensation being bathed; I had not had someone bathe me in a very long time.

I was deep in a relaxed state when her concerned voice broke the silence. 'Miss? Are you unwell?'

I opened her eyes and saw that her gaze was directed towards the water that had turned a pale shade of pink.

Looking up at her, I gave a reassuring smile. 'It is just the waning of the moon,' I lied. In households such as this, the help always gossiped and I knew they would be curious about me and the nature of my relationship with their master. I cared not what they thought of me, but I felt protective of Henry and did not want to provoke unnecessary speculation.

'Forgive me, Miss.' She lowered her head, ashamed at having prompted me to speak of such a private matter.

'Please think nothing of it.'

I stepped out of the tub while the girl fetched a warm towel from the airing cupboard and wrapped it around me.

She opened a door, revealing an adjoining dressing room. There were two other maids waiting for us when we entered. I took a seat on a small settee while they presented to me a selection of gowns. I wondered where they had come from; surely Henry did not have such items readily on hand for unexpected houseguests? Pushing these thoughts aside, I selected the one I liked best – a gown of gleaming olive green accented with pink satin and cream lace.

Removing the towel one of the girls lifted a clean chemise over my head, letting it glide down my ivory skin. I sat down at the dressing table. One of the girls brushed out my hair with a thick comb while another lavished on me powders, perfumes and rouge until I did not recognise the creature before me. My skin looked almost lifelike. More so than it had in the many months since I turned.

Next began the lengthy ordeal of dressing me. I was helped

into the many layers that were the custom of the day. Bloomers were added underneath my chemise and next a corset was laced over the top. The bounded sensation was new to me; I had never worn a corset as I always dressed myself and had never been shown how to lace myself in. The effect it had on my form was quite appealing. I was next helped into layers of petticoats and a crinoline. It was springtime so I did not require as many layers as the colder months would have required. Then they added a wired bustle in order to achieve the desired shape. Finally, I was helped into the dress itself.

One of the girls opened another cabinet and removed a pair of white lace gloves and a fan that had a very pretty oriental-looking design on it. Another opened a velvet box and brought over to me a pair of pink garnet earrings and a necklace. The third brought over two boxes: one contained a matching green hat with a pink satin ribbon while in the other was a pair of matching shoes.

Once they were satisfied I was appropriately accessorised, I was brought over to a wardrobe with three mirrors to admire the completed look. I looked like an aristocrat – that is to say, like a doll that had been brought to life.

I did not know what engagement we had that evening, nor did I care, for as long as it was to be spent in Henry's company it did not matter.

I was led from the room and down the hallway to the staircase I had ascended the night before. At the bottom Henry stood waiting for me. As I approached him he held out a cape for me and placed it over my shoulders, fastening it at the front.

Henry's fixed his brilliant blue eyes on mine.

'You look magnificent, Rose. I am truly honoured to have you on my arm this evening.' He raised my hand and gently placed a kiss upon it. 'I am committed to attending a ball this evening and could not get out of the obligation. I hope you do not mind accompanying me?'

I was a bit disappointed that we must spend the evening

surrounded by others, but did not let it show. I smiled. 'You are not concerned about being seen in public with me? I mean without my having a proper chaperone? Will people not talk?' It was almost unheard of for an unmarried lady to attend a social event with an eligible bachelor if they were not already engaged to marry.

'I have made arrangements for a member of my staff to act as chaperone. You will suffer no reputational risk in accompanying me, I can assure you of that.' He winked and the corner of his mouth curled up in a sideways smile.

'It is not my reputation I am concerned for, Henry, but yours,' I responded coyly. My words were true: what care had I for my reputation?

I did, however, have another concern. I had not fed properly in over two days. Henry's blood was only a mere appetiser and not enough to sustain me long term. I felt weak and my senses were dulled.

I had never had to manoeuvre in such a full-skirted dress before and was surprised that I managed to do so with as much elegance and grace as I did.

Henry helped me into the carriage and climbed in after me. Just as I was about to lean over and let him know of my need to feed, a lady joined us.

'Rose, this is Mrs Stanson. She will be your chaperone for the evening.' Henry gave me a wink when he said the word 'chaperone'. I could see he was having fun with this. However, my mood was less favourable. I was in no mood to play the gentlewoman this evening and sitting in such close proximity to him only made my hunger grow.

I could not help but think of the last uncomfortable carriage ride I had taken. I tried not to think of Mr Weir these days. When I did, I often felt a sadness come over me. But why? Had he not been a vile loathsome man who had deserved to die? So why did the very thought of him fill me with such melancholy? My mind was troubled and confused.

After a relatively short journey, we arrived at our destination, which was a private estate located on the outer edges of London. The surroundings were quite rural. The carriage passed through a large iron gate and continued towards the courtyard. In the indigo of the evening the windows radiated orange with lamplight.

Upon entering someone took our cloaks and hats and ushered the three of us into a grand ballroom. The room was buzzing with activity. I could feel studying eyes following me as we entered and the steady hum of speculative whispers.

Henry weaved through the crowd of people, nodding his head and acknowledging individuals as he did so. He stopped to exchange brief pleasantries with some, mainly about the weather or current affairs. I was introduced simply as 'Lady Rose' (although we both knew I was not really a lady) and there was no mention of the nature of our relationship.

We stood for some time watching the others dance and converse. I was bored and overtaken with hunger. The endless swirling of fabric and dense chatter was making me uneasy. I closed my eyes, trying for a moment to block out the symphony of sounds; I could smell their flesh, powdered and sweet. My teeth begin to grow and sharpen.

I could sense Henry draw nearer, his familiar scent filling my nostrils. I felt the tickle of his breath on my hair as he leaned in and whispered in my ear. 'Rose, take the next dance with me.'

Nodding, I opened my eyes and admired his appearance. He was wearing a well-tailored ebony dress jacket, waistcoat and trousers. His white shirt and collar were crisp and clean, and his bow tie was perfectly tied without a hint of lop-sidedness.

I looped my arm through his and let him lead me to the dance floor. We moved effortlessly together, perfectly synchronised as our eyes fixed on one another. His gaze was hypnotising and the world around us seemed to disappear.

Never before had I felt the depth of desire as I felt for this man. In such a short time he had consumed me. Sadness overcame me as I recalled my true nature. How long could this last? I pushed this thought out of my head; I did not want to think of the future, of what lay ahead for us.

Henry seemed to register my moment of melancholy and pulling me towards him whispered in my ear. 'Something troubles you. Will you not confide in me?' He pushed me away again while we turned.

When we were once more facing each other I shook my head and gave him a reassuring smile. 'You need not concern yourself. We shall speak privately when we are safe from prying ears.'

The music ended and Henry and I gave each other the customary bow. He was leading me towards our chaperone when a tall silver-haired gentleman approached Henry and said something in his ear. Henry nodded and addressed me, 'If you will excuse me for a brief moment, Rose, I must attend to something. I promise, I shan't be very long.'

'Very well, I shall do my best to stay out of trouble,' I teased. Although, with the way I was feeling I would very much have to try in order to control my urges.

I watched Henry exit the room while I stood next to my chaperone. I was growing impatient and hungrier by the minute and wished for Henry's swift return.

My eyes scanned the crowd and came into focus on a young gentleman walking towards me. At first I thought his attention must be fixed on someone nearby, but as he drew nearer and stood before me I could not deny I was the subject of his attention. I glanced at my chaperone, who seemed unconcerned that a gentleman was approaching me without first being properly introduced. I deduced that my chaperone was purely ornamental and would likely not so much as flinch if my petticoats were thrown up and I was mounted right there before her.

'I noticed your dance card is not yet full and it would please me if you would share the next dance with me.'

I was intrigued. Surely Henry would not mind; after all, we were not engaged and I was trying my best to blend in.

I took the gentleman's hand and obliged him in a dance. I learned that his name was William Lockhart, and that he was the son of a Scottish aristocrat. His manner was sweet and kind and his mastery of conversation was good even if from time to time he would grow crimson about his cheeks when I spoke. He escorted me across the room when the music stopped and returned me to my chaperone, bidding me farewell.

Once seated, I scanned the room to see if Henry had returned. Through the whirling couples I saw him sanding at the opposite side of the room. His bright blue eyes fixed on mine. I felt my stomach flutter with joy. Was such a reaction even possible for a creature such as I?

Henry's eyes remained on mine as the silver-haired gentleman continued to converse with him. Finally, begging to be excused, he crossed the room and sat down beside me.

'Mrs Stanson, would you be so kind as to leave Rose and me for a moment?' I could tell by the way he spoke that it was not so much of a request as an order.

Once Mrs Stanson had left the room Henry quietly addressed me. 'Watching you dance with another affected me in quite an unexpected way, Rose. I am ashamed to admit I felt quite troubled by the sight.'

'Henry, my love, how would it seem if I were to refuse a dance when my ball card was not yet full? You know very well that I was obliged to accept.'

'I suppose you are right. Still, I did not like how it made me feel. You have no idea how beautiful and enchanting you are. The way these men look at you… I only ask you to be careful. Now I must quickly fill up that card of yours with my name alone – sod propriety! I shan't share you with another this evening.' Henry gave me a wink and stood before me, the corners of his mouth drawn up into smile. He held out his hand and as I took it I knew we belonged to one another and to no one else.

The hour was late when we left the ball and began our journey home, but for me the day had barely just begun. I stared up at the tall white house from the carriage window. I had still not fed and feared what would happen if I returned inside that house with Henry. Was I really capable of harming him? For both our sakes I hoped not, but I was not willing to risk it.

Mrs Stanson stepped out of the carriage first and Henry moved to follow. I grabbed his shoulder to stop him and spoke as softly as I could into his ear. 'Henry, I cannot follow you into that house unless I have fed first.'

Henry turned and looked into my eyes. I could see he understood my sense of urgency, my fear. He told Mrs Stanson that she was no longer needed and ordered the driver to drive on. 'I know a place. They are discreet.'

I could not bear to look at him. I was ashamed of my dark need. Ashamed that he had to share in this side of me.

'Do no fret, my Rose. I will ensure you are safe and taken care of. What is it that you require… exactly? I only ask so that I may brief my acquaintance appropriately in my request.'

'I require blood, ample – fresh preferably.'

'That can be arranged. And no life need be taken in order to fulfil this need?' he asked timidly, as if not wishing to insult me.

'The taking of life is not necessary – but the longer I go without feeding the stronger the hunger is and the harder it is for me to control myself. To stop.' I turned and gave Henry a gentle smile. I did not want him to fear me; I only wanted him to understand the situation in full.

The carriage slowed as it pulled into the side of the street. Henry climbed out, helping me out after him. He took my hand and led me down a dark narrow passageway. In the dim lamplight the shadow he cast was long and thin before him.

We quickly arrived at a doorway over which showed a single red light. Henry lifted his hand and rapped loudly. The sound cut through the silence of the night like a hammer struck on a church altar.

The door opened and a woman stood before us. Her face was heavily painted – a mask of youth applied to her middle-aged skin. 'Georgie boy – 'ow lovely to see ya. Who's this sweet thing you brought me? Such a fair pretty little thing.' Her eyes scanned over me as if appraising my value; seeming satisfied, her red lips stretched into a large grin.

'Madam Sperling, a pleasure to see you looking so well. We are interested in the company of one of your girls.'

'Two girls, actually,' I corrected. If I was to avoid taking their life, I would need the blood of more than one.

The madam threw her head back and laughed. 'Interested in an education, are we? Well, if that's what yer after we've got the best educators outside of Paris. Come in and take your pick.' She led us inside. The interior was bright with lamplight and a grand staircase spiralled around a lofty space of at least four storeys. Hanging over the banisters the curious faces of girls of varying degrees of beauty and age stared down at us. Some looked even younger than myself.

After a brief scan I selected the two who looked the most sumptuous. 'That one there – and this one in the blue,' I pointed, whispering my preference in Henry's ear.

We were escorted upstairs to one of the vacant rooms. As I entered the small chamber, I looked back and observed Henry press a couple notes into the madam's outstretched palm. She winked at him in gratitude. I could not help but notice the familiar way Henry interacted with her. Before I turned, I would have found this place and Henry's knowledge of it shocking and distasteful, but after all I had seen, all I had been witness to, nothing much offended me.

Living in the East End, I had heard of such places as these, where upper-class men liked to come slumming with the lower classes. Is that what Henry was doing with me now – slumming?

Had he grown tired of what was currently on offer and had I whetted his appetite for something new, something dangerous?

'Rose, my pet, you look as though you are a million miles away.' Henry's words brought me back to the situation in hand. The two girls were already seated on the bed. Both were around eighteen years of age and the way their pale skin glowed pink in the lamplight made me believe that they were both fine specimens of good health.

Turning to Henry, I leaned in close so as not to be overheard, 'If you would rather, you can wait outside and make sure that no one disturbs us.'

'I would prefer to stay, but can move the armchair closer to the door so I can hear anyone approaching.' Henry leaned over and kissed me, reaching down he locked the door behind us.

'Very well then, as you wish.' I took off my hat and cape and passed them to Henry. I turned to face the girls, slowly freeing my fingers, one by one, from the fabric of my white gloves. I heard Henry drag the chair towards the door. The girls giggled to one another as I approached and parted to make a space between them for me to sit.

One of the girls had dark-brown hair which fell about her décolletage in large ringlets. Her eyes were a warm brown with flecks of green in them that gleamed as they caught the lamplight. The other was fair and blonde with ice-blue eyes. 'You are so beautiful, my little darling; so sweet, so innocent,' the brown-haired one lulled, caressing my arm. The other girl ran her long delicate fingers through my hair entangling them in my curls. I could feel her breath moist on my neck, smell the sweetness of her scent, and the sweetness of her blood.

They worked at unbuttoning my dress and unfastening the bustle and as I stood they lifted me up out of it and back on to the bed. Layers of crinoline puffed up around us like a fluffy white cloud concealing us momentarily from Henry's fixed gaze.

I was enveloped in a sea of soft milky white skin while they lavished me with kisses, spoilt me with their caresses. I could no longer resist my urge; I felt my fangs sharpen beneath my lips and sunk them into the exposed flesh of the brunette's bosom. She growned with delight as I sucked the warm red liquid from within her veins, careful not to spill a drop. Once I felt her heart begin to slow I stopped myself: she was unconscious but would live.

I turned and faced the other girl, who seemed oblivious to the condition of her companion. Without hesitation I got my fill of her as well.

When I lifted my head I saw that Henry was no longer seated but was standing before me. His eyes full of excitement and desire. I reached up and found his lips with my bloodied mouth and pulled him towards me. We made love quickly and fiercely, entangled between the two sleeping beauties.

Henry's head lay upon my stomach. His breath was heavy and deep. 'We should go before they wake, my love,' I said to him as I ran my fingers through his golden locks.

'Hmm... yes, I suppose we must. Will they not remember what transpired?' He glanced in the direction of one of the dormant girls.

'If they do, it will seem but a dream. They were heavily compelled and their marks have already healed – look... see.' I pulled back the hair of one of the girls to show him. My blood had the ability to heal the wounds of the living and by lacing the open wound with but a drop, it had ceased to bleed and closed before our eyes.

His eyes grew wide with curiosity.

I took his face in my hands. 'I know what you are thinking... I swear to you that I have never compelled you.'

'But why not?' he asked.

'For the same selfish reason you still bear the marks of my dark kisses; I want you to remember me – to look upon yourself and see me. Your marks are a token of what has passed between us.'

'Oh Rose! How could I ever forget you? Not even if God himself willed it could my arms forget the memory of your flesh warmed by my embrace; my lips not recall the softness of your kisses. You are my everything.'

I closed my eyes and kissed his forehead while inhaling his scent. It was comforting, like home. He was my calm within the storm. If only he knew how dark things could really be, how possible it was for him to one day wish to forget me... even beg for it. 'Come we must go, the day grows near.'

Henry and I were well on our way home when he asked the question I suspect had been on his mind since the first night we spent together.

'Rose, how did you come to be this way?'

'It was my destiny. I had no choice in the matter, I know that now. She who made me as I am has bestowed upon me a great gift, one with many advantages. But it is also a curse for it has cost a great price. I have lost my beloved father, my childhood, my innocence, and I have stolen the lives of others in order to sustain mine. For that I am most certainly damned.' I looked into his searching eyes and felt ashamed of what I was.

'I do not believe for a moment you are damned, as you say. You did not choose to become what you are. And if it was really destined to be then such was the will of God. For only he can decide the fate of man.' Henry pulled me towards him and held me tight.

'You think too well of me, Henry. I am not worthy of your goodness.'

'Shh, my sweet. You are a magnificent creature. How can you not see how truly special you are? If only my eyes were mirrors, that I could reflect in them to you your own benevolence.'

'Your esteem of me is too great and unwarranted – I fear it will not be long before I shall disappoint you.'

'I know what you are. I know what you are capable of. I see you, and that is how I know you are not as low a creature as you think you are. Let me show you how worthy you are.' He pulled me on to his lap and I fitted into him like a hand in an old glove.

'Come away with me to my country house, Rose. I have grown tired of London, of the Season, and wish to have you all to myself, away from all these tedious social engagements.'

'Of course, Henry, until the day you no longer wish it, wherever you go I shall follow.'

'Then you shall follow me till the end of time.'

Back at Henry's all was quiet inside. Still wrapped in his arms we ascended the stairs towards Henry's bedchamber.

I grew more and more tired as the dawn crept nearer. Henry helped me to undress, peeling the layers off slowly as if unveiling a sacred relic. I felt cherished. Lifting me back into his arms he placed me on the bed before setting to work on unfastening the shinny gold buttons of his jacket.

I sat up and looked at him. He truly was a very handsome man and I loved him ardently.

'How is it that I do I not frighten you? Not even I know what I am truly capable of.' I slipped off his jacket and began to unfasten his bow tie.

'To fear you would be like fearing myself. For no man truly knows what deeds they are capable of – or what darkness may lie at the very centre of their heart. What I do know is that I think of you every waking moment and I long for you when we are separated. How could this leave room in my heart for fear when I am so full already of my love and want of you?' Taking my face in his hands he kissed me.

I slipped his shirt over his head exposing his bare chest; his pale skin shimmered in the moonlight. He winced as I drew the first blood. I did not need to feed but I wanted to feel close to him, to feel his warmth within me. He wrapped his arms tight around me and entwined his fingers within my hair while inhaling deeply.

Henry drew the curtains as the first glimmer of dawn began to illuminate the darkness. He climbed into bed and then, almost as one, we drifted off into sleep.

My eyes fluttered open, adjusting to the dark interior of the blacked-out carriage. The wheels turned methodically below us. 'Where are we?'

'We are en route to my country house. We will arrive shortly. My apologies for whisking you away this afternoon while you slept. The journey is a difficult one to make under the cover of darkness and I could not bear the thought of spending another day in the city, when I could have you all to myself in the countryside. You don't mind, do you?' He caressed my head softly as I stretched out across his lap, like a purring feline.

'No, not at all. Although, I imagine the journey has been rather dull with no view to admire and no companion to converse with.' I reached out my hand and ran my fingers over the soft velvet curtains that were drawn across the window to block what remained of the daylight.

'On the contrary, I have had the most pleasing view to admire.' He leaned down and kissed me. His lips were soft and warm against mine. A copy of Tolstoy's *Anna Karenina* lay open across my chest. If I had not noticed the smell of a not-long-extinguished lamplight, I would have wondered how he could have read in such darkness.

I picked up the book and scanned the open page:

What would come of it all he did not know, he did not even think. He felt that all his forces, hitherto dissipated, wasted, were centred on one thing, and bent with fearful energy on one blissful goal. And he was happy at it. He knew only that he had told her the truth, that he had come where she was, that all the happiness of his life, the only meaning in life for him, now lay in seeing and hearing her...

'What is it about, this book you read?' I asked of Henry, closing the book and placing it down beside me.

'It is a love story, but a complicated one – as I suppose all true love stories are. This man, Count Vronsky, is loved by Kitty, a young pretty thing adored by many. But when Vronsky meets

Anna, a married aristocrat, he becomes infatuated with her and feels he must have her.'

'How interesting – I must know, does Anna return Vronsky's affection?'

'Oh yes, she is drawn to him in a way she can neither control nor deny, but she knows to accept his affection would bring great shame.'

'And does she eventually succumb?'

'I suspect she does. The moment she meets Vronsky she realises how little she cares for her husband. His very manner offends her. In Vronsky she sees something she cannot explain. Something which grabs a hold of her heart and won't let go.' Henry pulled me up into his arms and wrapped them tightly around me. 'I fear in the end their love will consume them.' The tone in which he spoke these words made me wonder if he was still speaking of Vronsky and Anna or of him and me.

'I think I would rather be consumed by love than to never truly know love at all,' I proclaimed, swinging my legs around to sit upon his lap.

The book fell to the floor. Henry's lips found mine again but this time they were more eager. He pulled the fabric down off my shoulders exposing my flesh to the cool air. His warm hands trailed over me. I shivered. In that moment I wanted nothing more than to be near to him; to feel his warmth pressed against my cool flesh; to have the metallic taste of his blood in my mouth; and to be consumed … by love.

'I believe we have arrived.' Henry pulled the curtain back and gazed out the window. We must have been travelling for several hours, as it was now nightfall. 'I cannot see much through the darkness but I recognise the familiar bend in the road. That must be the gate ahead.'

Unlike Henry, my eyes could see through the blackness and make out the scenery ahead as we approached. A large iron gate towered before us. Its hinges seemed to let out a long sigh as they were swung open by two of Henry's men.

As we rolled leisurely up the stony drive, I noticed a dozen or so glowing windows twinkling in the darkness like little dancing fairies. I had never before seen a place so grand.

'This is where you live? There must be dozens of rooms!' I exclaimed in disbelief.

'Some of the time I do, yes. But I'm afraid it does not really belong to me. My father has a love of acquiring property. This is just one of his many houses.'

'He must be very influential indeed to lay claim to something so grand and beautiful as this.'

'My father has no appreciation for beauty. For him it is an investment, like most things in his life.' The manner in which Henry spoke of his father was abrupt and cold and his tone gave no hint of affection.

'Forgive me.' I looked down self-reproachfully. 'It is not becoming to speak of wealth and grandeur – I have forgotten myself.'

'Rose, I wish for us to always be honest with one another. Never apologise for speaking what is on your mind. I have had my fill of proper ladies who speak only what they are told is appropriate and acceptable. I love that you speak your mind so freely. Do not let this place change that between us.' He brushed my hair away from my face and kissed me gently on the forehead then kindly wrapped a blanket around my shoulders.

The carriage rolled to a halt. Henry jumped out first. I admired the slow graceful way in which he moved, always in careful control of the space around him and the manner in which his limbs occupied it. When he secured his footing he reached for me and lifted me up into his strong firm arms. I felt like royalty as he carried me across the threshold into the grand foyer. The marble floor felt cool beneath me as my feet touched the ground.

A tall slender man approached us. He was dressed in a black

suit and crisp white shirt. His black hair had been slicked back in such haste that a small piece had begun to fall in front of his eyes.

Henry handed him his cloak and hat and then patted him on the back in a most jovial way.

'Henderson, you needn't have roused yourself to greet us.'

'Nonsense, Lord Henry. We were all quite excited to receive notice of your arrival. You must be ravenous. Shall I have kitchen prepare you something?'

'I have worked up quite the appetite, so I suppose I should. But I must insist that they do not go to too much trouble. Just some bread and wine will suffice.'

'For two?' Henderson asked, looking in my direction quizzically.

'What's that? Oh yes forgive me. This is Lady Rose. As my telegram explained, she will be staying with us.'

I saw that Henderson's eyebrow seemed to rise in disapproval, but as soon as Henry's eyes were on him he smiled and said, 'How lovely to have a young lady in the house to look after.' He turned and looked back at me, adding an extra ingratiating smile. 'Henry here struggles to keep us on our toes; he is so easy to look after.'

'Well, in future I will try and be more demanding, shall I?' Henry chuckled playfully. They were addressing each other on the most comfortable terms and you could tell that they had been long acquainted.

'Come let's get you dressed in something more substantial. This old house is draughty and I wouldn't want you to catch a chill.'

Henry took my hand and led me up the grand staircase. Once we were out of Henderson's earshot Henry turned to me. 'Most of the staff here are loyal to me but they are under the employ of my father and I often wonder if they report back to him of my coming and goings.'

'Understood, but surely if such is true, he will learn of my being here?'

'I imagine he already knows. Nonetheless we should try and give them as little to gossip about as possible.' He pulled the blanket further up around my shoulders and clasped it with his hand in front. I gazed up at him. 'This is going to be harder than I thought,' he said with a coy smile.

Henry led me down the hall and into one of the rooms. A lamp had already been lit. It was a dressing room. He walked over to one of the wardrobes and opened it.

'Let's see. This should do.' He pulled out a plain cream frock.

I dropped the blanket to the floor and raised my arms above me. Henry walked towards me pulled off my simple underlayer, and lifted the frock over my hands and let it fall over me into place. I ran my fingers over the fabric. There was a motif of leaves and flowers embroidered on it.

My eyes met Henry's; he was staring at me intently. 'Even in the simplest of attire you look stunning.'

If I were capable of blushing, I would have. I had never been admired in such a selfless and genuine way before.

He brought me over a pair of plain black boots. 'I know you won't really catch a chill – but for appearance's sake we can't have you running amuck in only your chemise and bare feet.'

I stepped into the shoes and watched as he laced them up one by one. The care he took in dressing me reminded me of a child dressing her doll. I suppose in a way to him I was like a doll.

Lastly, Henry draped the blanket back over my shoulders, leaning in and kissing me as he did so. His scent was sweet and intoxicating as it always was.

'Would you do me the honour of keeping me company while I dine?'

'Of course, Henry, I always wish to be near you.'

'Very well. Follow me.' Henry led the way: back down the never-ending hallways and the grand staircase, towards the rear of the house (if you could call it that) and finally into the dining room.

The table had already been set with two places towards the far end of the long room. Glowing under the flicker of candlelight was a carafe of wine with a platter of bread, cheese and a bunch of grapes.

This was the first time Henry and I had sat down to a meal together – usually it was me who was doing the feeding. Tonight I sat back and watched him as he sipped his wine and ate his bread. There was something sensual in watching him fulfil his human need for sustenance. He poured more of the dark-red wine into his glass. He saw me eyeing it. 'Would you like me to pour you a glass?'

'No, I would rather taste its afterglow.'

He took another sip; a drop of wine spilled from his mouth and trickled down his lip. I leaned forward and kissed him, wiping away the trickle of wine with my tongue. His breath was hot upon my skin. 'It tastes sweet, like you.'

Someone cleared their throat behind us. 'I beg your pardon, Sir, I was just coming to check if you would be requiring anything more this evening?'

In the doorway stood a round portly woman with grey hair peeking out from beneath her white bonnet. Her face was stern and I saw little evidence of joy in her, as if she had scarcely smiled all her life.

'No, that will be all, Mrs Motts.'

She fixed her stern eyes on mine and did not break eye contact with me as she spoke. 'Very well, Sir, then I bid yous goodnight.'

I could not help but break out in a fit of laughter as she took her leave of us. 'What a horrible old woman. Did you see the way she looked at me – as though I was something she had accidentally dragged in on her boot?'

Henry returned my laughter and dragged me on to his lap. 'She is not all that bad. I have known her since I was a boy. She used to sneak me sweeties between meals...' He smiled to himself as if remembering a moment from his youth. 'She just needs to adjust to having you around.'

'Well, I suppose you know your staff best but it seems to me that they are not entirely pleased to have me here.'

'Not much changes around here. Most of them have been here for decades. They are not sure what to make of you, but give them time. They will warm to you eventually.' Henry held me tight against him. 'Shall we retire to bed?'

'Yes, let's.' I brushed my cheek against his. My own hunger was beginning to grow again.

We climbed the stairs back up to the second floor. He led me again down the long hallway.

'This room is mine,' he said, opening the door. He looked around to make sure no one was looking before leading me across its threshold. Henry lit a candle and walked towards another door located on the right wall of the room. 'This door here leads to your room.'

I did not understand. 'Will we not be sharing a bed?' I felt a pang of longing as I spoke the words.

'Of course we will. But this way when I rouse you can be left to sleep undisturbed. I will instruct the staff not to enter your room until nightfall.' He opened the door to the adjoining room and placed the candle on a small table beside a large canopy bed. 'Do you think I could really sleep one wink without you in my arms?'

He walked slowly towards me while removing his jacket and throwing it on to a nearby chair.

I looked into his eyes and reaching up I ran my fingers through his tousled hair. 'Well, then take me into your arms, lover, for I am yours to embrace.'

Henry wrapped his arms around my waist. It was a familiar feeling I had grown so used to over the past couple days. I rested my head on his chest and listened to his slow gentle breath. 'Henry...'

'Yes, Rose?'

'I think I may be falling in love with you.'

'Well, then let me catch you,' Henry said as he swooped me up into his arms and took me to bed.

CHAPTER 6

Henry lay fast asleep beside me. My eyes scanned the darkness. I had tried to force myself to be still – to quieten my mind – but I was a creature of the night, nocturnal, so I lay awake. I knew that when the dawn came that the heaviness would overcome me and I would feel the urge to sleep. Until then I had a couple of hours before the twinkling stars would begin to fade.

I untangled my limbs from the heap of our embrace and slipped silently out of bed. Henry did not stir. He looked so peaceful when he slept. His dishevelled golden curls lay about his youthful face in such a way as to make him look almost angelic. As if he had fallen from the heavens.

I quickly pulled on my boots and laced them haphazardly, throwing the blanket once again over my shoulders before exiting the room. The house was still. The staff would soon be waking to begin their daily duties. In a house as grand as this it must take many people to keep things running efficiently. Silently I made my way down the main staircase and towards the rear of the house.

I entered one of the rooms. It was furnished with a grand piano and two small settees. In the silence I could almost hear the melodic stroking of fingers on the keys.

The rear wall was lined with a series of windows and a set of doors that led outside.

It was a cool damp night. I closed my eyes and inhaled the night air. The grounds on Henry's estate were overwhelmingly vast. I cared not for his wealth and title. To me he was just Henry, but I could not help but wonder how long it would be before it would matter to him. Was his interlude with me just a fleeting thing? I knew we could never be married. God cannot join the damned nor can the bodies of the dead bring forth life. All I could ever be to him was his mistress, the fulfiller of his most carnal desires.

I wandered the grounds until at last I could sense the approaching dawn and so I returned to the house.

On my way back through the house I heard someone stirring. I turned around and saw Mrs Motts, the cook, sticking her head out of a small room.

'Morning, Miss. Where're you comin' from at this hour?' She looked at me disapprovingly; I was still only wearing my thin white chemise and a blanket.

'I could not sleep and thought some fresh air might do some good,' I answered.

'Hmm. Not my place to say, I suppose – but a young lady should not be wandering about in only her under-things, restless or otherwise.' She crossed her arms in front of her overly sized bosom. She had a hard look about her as if she had been in service for many years.

'No, it is not your place to say, so you would be wise to be silent!' I snapped. 'Now if you will excuse me, I was just on my way back to bed.' I turned and began to walk away.

I was almost at the landing when she called out to me. 'Lord Henry is betrothed you know. They are to be married in a couple of weeks. His father, the Duke, arranged it himself so you'd be wise not to go messing things up.'

Within seconds I had forced her back into the room out of which she had stuck her nosy little head.

'You would be best to keep your mouth shut,' I warned.

'I shan't be taking orders from a little ginger whore. Now get your hands off of me.'

Her words sent me over the edge. I could no longer control my dark urge. I sunk my teeth into her neck. Only this time when I heard the sound of heart beginning to slow I did not stop. I drained that cow dry.

I extracted my teeth and I let her body fall to the ground with a thud. Her vacant eyes stared up at me. Her mouth contorted into a permanent look of horror. What had I done?

I was in quite a predicament for I had a body to dispose of but the dawn was quickly approaching. I had to act quickly. I threw her over my shoulder and quickly ran from the house. With fresh blood coursing through my veins my strength and speed were at their best. Dropping her body down just beyond the treeline I examined the scene. I needed to make her wounds look more savage, like an animal attack. I bent over her and ripped into the already present wounds, this time roughly tearing at the flesh.

I was covered in blood. I could not return to the house like this. I scanned my surroundings and saw a small pond. That would have to do. I submerged myself in the water and washed away the blood and filth from my face and hands. Once I was sufficiently clean, I hurried back to the house and managed to make it inside Henry's bedroom just as the sun peeked out from beneath the horizon.

I stripped off the soaking-wet garments and boots and climbed into bed, pulling the bed-curtains closed.

I curled into Henry's warmth. He stirred. 'Rose. Is that you? Were you gone?' He pulled me closer and wrapped his leg around me.

'Hush, my darling. I am here.' I was too tired to speak more. We had much to discuss but now was not the time. Slumber called.

CHAPTER 7

'Rose, Rose, wake up,' Henry called; I could feel his hands on my shoulders shaking me awake.

I opened my eyes; it was daylight still. 'What hour is it?' My body was heavy with tiredness and it took great effort to sit up.

Henry looked dishevelled and had dark circles around his glistening blue eyes. 'It is late afternoon. Sorry to wake you but I have just spent the afternoon with the Constable – Mrs Motts' body, was found late this morning by the groundskeeper. One of the girls thought it odd that preparations for breakfast had been started but seemingly abandoned and Josephine who shared a room with her said she had risen at her regular hour this morning but she had not seen her since. It was not long after that her body was found near the edges of the forest.' Henry was sitting on the edge of the bed with his back to me. He was visibly shaken.

'She said you are to be married. Is it true?' I knew he suspected I was responsible for Mrs Motts' death and that he wanted an explanation from me, but I needed to know the truth first.

Henry turned to look at me. He had been crying, but the tears had been wiped away. 'Yes, it is true. Did she explain that it is Father's wish that I marry Dora, not mine?'

'Not in so many words. She insisted that I leave you alone. She called me a whore – I may have overreacted.'

'Overreacted? You tore her bloody throat out! Jesus Rose, do you not have any self-control?' Henry looked at me with shock and disdain; it hurt.

'Henry, please do not look at me that way; you know what

I am. I am trying very hard to control my urges but what she said…' I took Henry's face in my hands and made him look at me. 'Do you not know how deeply I love you? To learn you belonged to another was the greatest injury anyone could inflict.' I kissed his lips hard. When I pulled away his face was stained with my bloodied tears.

'Rose, you're crying blood.' He pulled a white cotton handkerchief from his pocket and wiped away my tears. When he was done I returned the gesture.

In that moment I felt shame for what I was, for what I had done. How had I come so far from the girl I had once been? I was so far removed from the innocent I had been now; there was only darkness. Henry was the only glimmer of light that remained, my redeemer.

He placed a soft kiss on my forehead. 'I will let you sleep a bit longer, my love. It is not yet sundown. I've taken the liberty of burning your soiled garments in the fire, no one should ever know it was you.'

I lay back down, 'Thank you Henry. Will you not lay beside me for a little while?' I asked, hopeful we could put the day behind us together.

'I am afraid I have matters to attend to. The Constable has only just left and the body is being removed from the premises. I will come back for you at sundown.' Henry rose and pulled the bed-curtains around the bed, stopping just before they were fully closed. 'Sweet dreams, my dark angel.' He closed the curtains shutting out the dwindling light of day.

I woke a short while later, alone in the cold dark room. The house was silent.

Rising from the bed I pulled a blanket over my naked flesh. My skin was itchy from the muddy pond water and I could smell traces of blood still imbedded in the folds of my flesh.

Opening the door, I looked out. Henry had not returned and no one had come to get me.

I made my way down the hallway to the bathroom. It was empty but a bath had been drawn. I dipped my hand in the water – it was still warm. I let the blanket fall to my feet and climbed in. The water slowly turned a murky shade of grey. I closed my eyes and leaned my head back. The look of horror on Henry's face haunted me. Would he ever forgive me? Could he?

When I was sufficiently clean I drained the tub and wrapped myself in a large towel and headed in search of the ladies' dressing room.

I had begun opening doors and looking within when I heard someone call to me from the other end of the hall.

'There you are, Miss Rose, I just went to fetch you for your bath but I see you have already seen to it yourself.'

A maid came and put her arm around me directing me further down the hall. 'Come on then, this way. Let's get you dressed, before you catch a chill.'

Once I had been dressed I was told that dinner would be ready shortly and I was free to do as I wished until that time. I thought of Mrs Motts' discarded bloodied corpse; I wondered who would be preparing the meal.

The house was very grand and had more closed doors than I could count. Surely Henry must be behind one of them.

When I had had no luck locating Henry on the ground and first floors, I continued the search on the third floor. Many of the doors on this level were locked. At last I came to a door at the far end of the house. I turned the knob, it did not resist and the door slowly swung open. The room was warm and illuminated by the soft glow of a fire.

For a moment I thought I saw the familiar sight of Mr Weir sitting in his chair in front of the fire holding a glass of amber-coloured liquid. I closed my eyes and when I reopened them I saw Henry look up from his glass.

I stood in the doorway unmoving, unsure if he wanted me to enter.

'Come here,' he instructed boldly.

I went to him and kneeled before him, placing my head in his lap. I could not bear to look at him directly. It was not that I was ashamed or regretful for what I had done, but I had been careless and had put Henry in harm's way.

'I am not mad at you, Rose. I have been thinking about what I would do if someone told me you belonged to another, if they tried to keep me from you. And while I may not have reacted in quite the same way, I understand the hurt that that must have caused you. I understand it because I love you too.'

I looked up at him. 'You love me still?'

'Yes, Rose, I love you still. I know you have certain impulses which cannot always be controlled and if I am to accept you as you are I must accept them too.'

'I do try, you know – to be good. But I cannot always play the part of the gentlewoman. It is exhausting! Even in my mortal life I found it tiresome. And now that it is no longer required of me I find myself forced into pretending to be something I am not.'

'I understand, Rose. Do you not think I grow weary of all my public obligations; the expectations that come with being the son of one of the wealthiest men in England? I am expected to act in a certain way at all times. But with you it is different: I do not feel the need to guard myself, I feel free. So how could I ask anything other than that from you?'

'Have I put you in any danger – do they suspect foul play?'

'As far as everyone is concerned it was an animal attack. I doubt we will ever hear of it again.'

'And you are not getting married?'

'No, Rose, I am not. I will be speaking with my father tomorrow to seek permission to call off my marriage.' He took a swig from his glass and put it down on the table beside him.

'Why does he want you to marry this woman anyway? Surely it is your choice whom you marry.'

'If you knew who my father was you would understand. He

is headstrong and he does nothing in life that he will not gain from. He treats me as if my life were not my own. I doubt he will understand my giving up a good match for someone he has never heard of. He will want to know every detail about you, your parentage and status, what lessons you have had, the size of your dowry.'

'But I am no one, a ghost. I do not really exist in this mortal world; I have no ties to it.'

'If you feel comfortable sharing with me a few basic details of your life, your proper name for instance, I will be able to see where we need to embellish the facts.'

'Very well, allow me to properly introduce myself.' I smiled. It was odd that, after all we had been through; we really knew so little about one another. 'When I lived I was called Kirstin Rose Elizabeth. My father was William James Maines; he died when I was nine. Our home was Blythewood in Essex and until his death I received a proper education befitting a young lady. After that my mother and I fell into destitution and I doubt whether there will be any record of us beyond that point.'

'Your mother, does she live?' he asked curiously.

'My mother is of no concern. She is an unfortunate creature and as far as I am concerned she may as well be dead.'

'Understood. And you yourself were never engaged to marry?'

'There was a man once who wished to make me his. But he was already married and sought only to make me his whore.'

'And did he succeed?' His voice was hard. I could feel the jealously rising within him.

'Do you really wish to know?'

He was silent for a moment, as if contemplating whether he really did wish to know, or if it would be better not to. Finally having made his decision he spoke: 'Yes.'

'No, but he was a very cruel man who did not take refusal easily. Sometimes when I close my eyes I can still see his face, still feel his hands upon me...' It had been so long since I had thought about

Mr Weir, about that night he had tried to rape me. 'You are the only man I have ever known.'

'I did not mean to upset you. Please forgive me for making you dredge up so many dark memories.' Henry pulled me up into his lap and placed a gentle kiss on my forehead. 'I will never let anything bad happen to you. You are safe now.'

'Before I met you I was unsure if I would ever feel safe again. You would never have a peaceful sleep again if you had witnessed half the horrors I have seen … the things I have done.' I looked upon Henry's face: his eyes were wide with recollection. Of course he had seen. I wondered if he had ever seen a dead body before that morning.

'I'm sorry – I can't stop picturing her. I have known her my whole life and now she's gone.'

'Do not be sorry, be proud that you still have enough goodness in you to mourn her. You are a good man, Henry,' I said, taking his face in my hands. 'I worry that I will steal that from you, your goodness. Then you will no longer be the Henry I know and care for.'

'Shh, do you not see how you have saved me? Before you there was a void within me, a space so dark and deep I sought anything to fill it. The moment I first saw you, it was as if the void began to fill. I was drawn to you in a way I have never been drawn to another. I knew in that moment we were destined to be together.' He pressed his lips hard against mine. 'All I want in this world is you. You are my every thought, the subject of every dream. You are the sun which lights my dark and dreary days. Without you I am empty.'

'Oh, Henry, I feel the same way but that does not change what I am.'

'I care not, I accept you for what you are and I will never again behave as I have done this morning.' He wrapped his arms around me and we sat entwined in front of the warmth of the fire. As I listened to the rise and fall of his chest and the gentle beating of his heart I let myself fall into him, giving way to love.

CHAPTER 8

The next morning Henry left for London to confront his father. When I woke that evening he had still not returned.

The wait was agonising and when I could no longer sit still with my thoughts I decided to take a walk. The night was dark and the pale moon was but a sliver in the sky. If I was to avoid killing any more of Henry's staff I needed to feed.

Moving swiftly into the woods, I sat perched behind a tree and listened to the noises of the night. A cacophony of scurrying and buzzing filled my head. I began to filter out the many layers of noise and focused in on the sound of the soft steps of an approaching doe. She did not sense me, but moved with caution.

I lowered myself closer to the ground and when it was safe to do so I pounced on the doe, sinking my teeth into her soft fuzzy neck. As her heartbeat began to fade she slowly sunk to the ground, drifting into an eternal slumber.

Is that all I had been to my maker, a meal? Now was not the time for such sombre thoughts. I decided to return to the house to see if Henry had returned from his journey and what news he had.

Removing my muddied boots before crossing the threshold I entered the house and made my way towards the stairwell. I needed to wash and change my clothes.

But just as I reached the bottom step Henry came barrelling through the front door. He tossed his hat and gloves at the butler, who looked surprised by Henry's abrupt entry.

'Rose, I must speak privately with you at once!' Henry called, as he sped up the stairs two at a time, leading me by the arm behind him.

I still had my muddy shoes and stockings in my hand and the sensation of my bare feet against the rough weave of the stair carpet was unpleasant.

Once inside the sitting room Henry shut the door behind us and immediately poured himself a drink.

I dared not speak; I had never seen him so angry.

'What a stubborn impossible man!' he shouted. 'It is my life to do with as I please yet he treats me like an insolent child.' He took a long sip of his drink, closing his eyes as he did so as if trying to make the world vanish for a moment.

'What happened? What did he say?' I asked. I knew it could not be good.

'I asked that he allow me to break off my engagement to Dora Mina, and he refused. I told him he had no right to refuse me, that it was my choice. You know what he said? You know what he had the audacity to say?' I knew that the question was merely rhetorical so I let him continue. 'He said that if I went against his wishes and called off the engagement he would cut off all financial support.' Henry sat down and put his head into his hands dragging them roughly back through his hair.

'And what did you say?' I asked quietly. It pained me to see him so upset.

He pushed him self up and began to pace the room. 'I told him to go to hell! I told him that I loved another and that I would not be forced to marry someone I did not care for.' He poured himself another drink and immediately drank it back in one gulp. 'And do you know what he said to me? What he had the nerve to propose? He said that if I was wise I would marry Dora and that I should take you as my mistress. Leave the whore a whore, he said. Leave the whore a whore!'

His words, although they were not his own, cut through me like a knife. I turned away from him, forcing down the urge to scream. When I had regained my composure I faced him.

'Henry, your father does have a point. I am not a suitable

match for you. I have nothing to offer you. We could never marry. God would not allow it for in his eyes I have turned my back to him. Our bond could only ever be as good as our word.' I paused for a moment. Henry placed his glass down and walked towards me. 'Henry, I think you should do as your father says. I refuse to let you be subjected to a life of ruin.'

He wrapped his arms around me. 'I would happily give up everything for you, Rose, and I do not need God's approval to know that my heart is bound to yours for eternity.'

'I know you feel that way now, but I ask that you at least think on it some more before making your decision.' I reached up and brushed the hair from his sad blue eyes.

'My mind is made up. I plan to speak with Dora myself and explain the situation to her. Surely she will not wish to marry a man whose heart belongs to another.'

'If that is what you think you should do, then I will not stop you. But do not be surprised if she will not give you up so easily. No woman I have known would willingly give up a man so worthy of marriage as yourself.'

'It matters not. I will not marry her!' Henry proclaimed, and I knew in that moment that he meant it.

CHAPTER 9

The rain came and stayed for several days. The roads were muddy and slick and were not ideal for travel. Henry wanted to speak to Dora in person. He did not feel a letter would suffice, believing that he would be better able to persuade her in person. Even if he could not admit it to himself, I knew he was scared. He was about to give up everything, his wealth, his home, his staff who had become like family to him, who helped raise him.

We rarely left the house and spent long hours in bed indulging in the sweetness of love. In those moments we spoke nothing of his engagement or the wishes of his father. The world seemed to disappear as if there were only he and I.

In order to control my hunger Henry gave me permission to hunt on his grounds. Sometimes he would send the carcasses that were suitable for human consumption down to the kitchens.

When the weather finally cleared we returned to London.

I was glad to be back in the city. I missed the familiar buzz, the scurrying people, the potential meals…

But sill he did not go to her. Instead he took to wandering the streets of the East End slums with me. Under the veil of darkness and mist he would assist me in seeking out healthy morsels to feed on, and then would keep guard while I fed. I was careful not to drain my victims fully. There was, of course, the odd one who was not so lucky. Henry seemed not to mind, and I worried he was beginning to lose himself in my dark world.

We spoke of taking a trip to Paris; he wanted to show me the preparations that were being made for the Grand Exhibition. He had read of an iron tower being constructed that was so tall it would surpass the spires of Notre-Dame. Life was good and I had nearly forgotten about our predicament until one night when the world decided it was time to remind us.

Henry and I had been to the opera and had only just returned. In our haste and greedy desire for one another we barely made it up the stairs before beginning to undress one another. Taffeta and silk scattered the hallway leading towards our room and behind the closed door Henry and I lay entwined, a web of limbs and glowing flesh.

We were just dozing off when there was a knock at the door. Henry called out, 'Who is it? It is late and I have retired to bed!'

There was no reply. We assumed that whoever it had been had decided against disturbing us. A moment later the door flew open and a tall well-dressed man entered the room. I could tell by the way he carried himself that he was a man of great importance.

He did not avert his gaze when he saw we were in bed together; instead, he passed his eyes over my nude form as if memorising every hill and valley. If I had been a shy woman, I certainly would have covered myself at once, but I had become accustomed to the studying gazes of men.

'Father! What is the meaning of this intrusion?' Henry shouted, covering himself hastily.

'Get dressed! I must speak with you at once.' Henry's father turned to leave, not waiting for agreement or response. Before he crossed the threshold he turned and called back, 'Leave the whore. My words are for your ears alone.'

Henry rose and quickly pulled on his dressing gown. 'Forgive me, Rose, I must go to him. He is an unreasonable man who does not take kindly to being kept waiting.' Henry gave me a quick kiss on the forehead before taking leave of the room.

After a short while alone I decided I could no longer sit and wait for his return. Why should I? The matter they were discussing most certainly concerned me. I began to dress and made my way out of the room to find them.

I was worried about Henry. Despite what he said, I could see from the brief interaction that his father held great influence over him.

Descending the stairs I followed their voices. Before entering the room I paused to listen in. His father was reprimanding him. 'You have disappointed me greatly, Henry. You have disobeyed my wishes, and what is worse, you have done so in public. Imagine my embarrassment to be surprised by the news that you were back in London and that you are traipsing around with a girl who is not your fiancée!' He was furious.

'Father, it is my life and I have the right to keep whatever company I please! I do not need your approval.'

'You have no right to publicly keep the company of a whore! Not while you are living under my roof and not while you carry my name!' The Duke slammed his fist against something, a table perhaps.

'She is no whore. Rose is perfectly respectable, Father. Why will you not just give her a chance?'

'Is that what you call what you two were doing in your chamber, respectable? This girl is not what she seems, Henry. I have asked around and no one seems to know who she is. What they do know is that she has been seen on the arm of more than one high-society man in London. Do you not see that she is only after your money? I beg of you, please do not continue this indecent liaison. If it is women's company you seek, visit a whorehouse!'

His words hurt me. Although what he said was mostly true, I cared nothing for Henry's wealth.

'For the last time, Father, she is no whore! I pursued her, not the other way around. I am the one who took her virtue. If there has been any seduction or corruption here, it has been by me. If I do not marry her, I will have ruined her reputation forever!' I heard the sound of something smash against a wall inside the room and decided that was my cue to intervene.

Without knocking, I opened the door and entered the room.

'Forgive my intrusion but as this conversation is about me I feel I have the right to be a part of it.' I walked over to Henry and gave him a soft kiss on the lips. I took his hand and coaxed him to sit down beside me.

The Duke looked at me with distaste. 'Very well, you appear to have great influence over my son, young woman, so maybe you can help me convince him he is making a grave mistake.'

'Forgive me, Sir, but we have not formally been introduced. If I am to speak freely with you, I feel as though proper introductions should be made.' I knew very well who he was but I needed him to know I was not beneath properly making his acquaintance.

Henry looked up as if awakening from his thoughts. 'Father, this is Kirstin Rose Elizabeth Maines, daughter of William James Maines of Blythewood Manor. Rose, this is my father, the Duke.'

'If we are finished with the formalities, I ask that we return to discussion of the matter at hand. As you are aware, Miss Maines, my son is engaged to marry another. The engagement is something I have arranged myself and it is a good match, one that I would not like to see broken. As I have explained to my son, if he chooses to go against my wishes he will no longer be welcome in my home and he will be cut off from all income that he himself has not earned.'

'Yes, Henry has fully explained the situation to me.' I took Henry's hand in mine and squeezed it gently. 'The way I see it is this, what Henry decides to do is his decision to make. I cannot tell Henry what to do any more than you can. Marriage is a sacred agreement between two people and should not be entered into lightly.'

'You are a woman and I could not expect you to understand the complex nature of the world we live in. One cannot simply choose to not do something because it is unpleasant or because he prefers something else. Do you think Adam had a choice in his union to Eve? Do you think Adam ever doubted the will of God?' The Duke grinned – he was clearly pleased with his cleverness.

I turned to Henry and raised his chin so his eyes met mine. 'Henry, my love, could I have a moment alone with your father?' I looked back at the Duke. 'That is, if the Duke will permit it?'

'Yes, my son, you may be excused. I am interested in what this silly girl has to say to me, and why it must be done in private.'

Henry looked drained; I could tell he did not have the energy to fight any longer. He got up and silently left the room. When the Duke and I were finally alone I turned to him. 'You may intimidate your son but I do not fear you. I will not bend so easily to your will.'

'Very well, speak your piece and be done with it.' The Duke lit a cigarette and sat down in the seat opposite me.

'Have you ever heard of Lilith, Sir?'

'The name is familiar but I do not see what relevance it has.' He inhaled a long drag and flicked the loose ashes on to the floor.

'Lilith was Adam's first wife but, unlike his second wife, Eve, who was created from the rib of Adam, Lilith was created from the same earth as Adam and stood by his side as his equal. Adam did not like that they were equal in the eyes of God; he wanted Lilith to be his subordinate, a plaything to pander to his every whim. Eventually Lilith left Adam and the Garden of Eden. It was then that God created Eve, who was a far more suitable wife for a man such as Adam.' I paused for a moment and looked deeply into the Duke's eyes. 'Let me ask you this. Do you think Lilith would have ever trusted that vile serpent? Do you think for one moment Lilith would have eaten that apple?'

The Duke sat back in his chair and crossed his right leg over his left resting his chin upon his hand. 'Interesting, so just to clarify, are you insinuating that Adam was indirectly responsible for the original sin?'

'All I am saying is that if men wish women to be subordinate to them, to be incapable of thinking for themselves, then they cannot very well hold them responsible for their actions.'

'It seems I have underestimated you. You certainly have a way about you that I find most intriguing, I can see why my son is so enamoured by you. That said, my opinion on the matter remains unchanged.'

I could see that no amount of words would ever persuade him to break off the engagement. His ego was far too strong to allow the risk of further damage to the family reputation. I let out a long sigh, I would have to tell Henry that the choice was his and that I would stand by him no matter what he decided to do; even if that meant him losing all the comforts he had become accustomed to.

'Thank you for your time and for allowing me to speak my piece. I love your son very much and do not wish to see him unhappy. Whatever choice he makes I will support it. If his choice is to marry Dora, rest assured that I will not stand in his way.'

The Duke looked at me in silence as if in deep contemplation. I had nothing further to say, but dared not leave until I had been excused. To my relief he broke the silence. 'I shall make you a deal. If Henry can persuade his fiancée to call off the engagement without causing upset to herself or her parents, then I will give you both my blessing. The hour is quite late and I must be leaving. I trust you will relay my proposition to my son?'

I nodded in agreement and he rose indicating that our conversation had at last come to an end. I stood and curtsied, and when I lifted my head our eyes met. 'You really are something else, my dear, a rare beauty. In my younger days I may have been tempted to steal you away and have you all to myself.' He took my hand and raised it to his lips; they were warm and soft against my cool hard flesh. I felt a rush of warmth to my face and closed my eyes. When I opened them he was gone.

When I woke the next evening Henry was no longer beside me. I had told Henry of his father's new proposal, which seemed to give him a new sense of hope. His mood had seemed to improve at once and we had even made love again before finally giving way once again to sleep.

Sitting up I pushed the blankets off of me. It was then that I noticed the note on Henry's pillow:

My dearest Rose,

I have gone to speak with Dora regarding our engagement. I shall, I hope, have returned by the time you wake – even as you lay here asleep I feel the pain of separation from you. I will hurry back with what I hope shall be the very best of news.

The moments I spend separated from you are the darkest hours of my day.

Ever yours,

H.

I held the paper over my heart, which if it were beating would surely have fluttered. He did love me, and I knew better than anyone that love could be a dangerous thing.

There was a knock at the door and the lady's-maid called out to me: 'Miss Rose, I ran a you bath.' It was a familiar routine, and she was right on schedule. I rose and followed her down the hall to the bathroom. One of the other maids was just finishing filling the tub. When it was ready I disrobed and climbed inside. The water felt warm and comforting.

A moment later I heard Henry's voice calling for me through the door. 'Rose, are you in there?'

'Yes, Henry, I'm in the bath. Come in, won't you?' I responded, eager to hear how things had gone with Dora.

Without hesitation he entered the room. The maids looked at me disapprovingly. I cared not; they all knew that our relationship was an intimate one so we might as well stop trying to pretend otherwise.

'Will you leave us, please; I must speak with Rose privately.' The girls did as he asked, leaving us alone.

Henry sat down on the small wooden stool beside me. He picked up a sponge and dipped it into the water; lifting it he squeezed the water over me. His manner was so gentle, so soothing. After a few minutes of silence he began to speak. 'Dora has requested to speak with you. I told her I did not think that was a good idea but she has insisted. I will understand if you refuse.'

I could understand why she wanted to see me. If I was about to lose my man to another woman, I would want to meet her too. 'So she has refused to break off the engagement without first speaking to the other woman involved? I must say she is more strong-willed than everyone makes her out to be.' I lay back and submerged my head under the water. I could hear his muffled voice through the water.

As I lifted my head from the water his voice became clear. 'So will you agree to meet her?'

'I agree, although I don't see how any good will come of it.' I placed my hands on his shoulders and slipped off his overcoat. One by one I undid the many buttons, peeling back each layer of clothing and letting them fall to the ground.

Without a word he finished undressing and climbed into the tub in front of me. He leaned back into me and I wrapped my legs around his waist. My flesh looked transparent like Japanese rice paper in comparison to his peachy tone.

I began to wash his hair, making cups of water with my hand and pouring them over his golden locks. When the water grew cool and Henry's skin began to wrinkle he lifted himself from the tub and walked over to the cupboard where the linen was kept. I admired the view from where I lay; he truly was a beautiful specimen. Wrapping a towel around his waist he brought another one over to me. I stood and allowed him to wrap the soft flannel around me as he lifted me out of the tub.

I rested my forehead against his chest and closed my eyes; his arms wrapped around my shoulders and squeezed me gently. I could be happy here forever ... he was my everything. I looked up at him and gave him a soft kiss. His brilliant blue eyes stared down at me. He kissed me again, this time separating my lips with his tongue. He tasted sweet.

He pushed against me. I sat against the edge of the tub and pulled the towel loose from his waist. I felt my fangs sharpen at the sight of him.

I let the towel fall from my shoulders; it gathered around my waist cascading down over the tub's porcelain edge. I felt his eyes drape over me full of desire.

'I love you so much. I fear at times my love for you will consume me,' he said.

'I love you too, Henry. You are my everything, my always … forever,' I professed, and then he was buried safe inside me.

We lay together on the cool marble floor of the bathroom. I kissed the top of his head taking in his scent; he smelled of sunlight. My hunger stirred, but I resisted the urge to drink from him. I wanted to feel normal, to feel human. The thought of meeting Henry's fiancée made me weary. How could I ever compete with the love of a mortal girl? I was nothing more than a monster hiding behind a cleverly designed facade, one that was devised to deceive and draw you in. How long before Henry tired of my wickedness and craved for something simple, something pure?

Was my influence over him so great that he could no longer think clearly? Why else had he not spoken to me of his engagement? Why had he kept such secrets?

Henry sat up and leaned against the tub. He seemed to sense my change in mood. 'This is all my doing. I have caused you unhappiness and for that I shall never forgive myself.' He ran his fingers through his hair. 'You must understand that it was not my intention to deceive you, Rose. From the first moment I saw you I knew I had to have you; everything else seemed to disappear. It was as if nothing else in the world mattered as long as I was with you.'

Lifting myself from the floor I curled into his lap. 'We all have secrets, parts of our life we wish to keep hidden in the shadows.' I grazed the tips of my fangs against his bare chest, and he shuddered. 'Do not apologise for causing me pain – it is an inevitable consequence of love. My heart will mend, though it may bear many scars by the time this whole ordeal is behind us once and for all.' Sinking my teeth into his chest I drank. I could hear his heart beating rapidly, as it struggled to meet the increased demand for blood.

Now both of our hearts would hurt.

CHAPTER 10

The next evening I was to receive Henry's fiancée. Henry assured me that she had been quite understanding when he spoke to her the previous day and simply wished to make my acquaintance before officially calling their engagement off. Men do not always fully understand the intentions of women.

When Dora finally arrived she was shown into the downstairs drawing room where Henry and I were sitting together on the settee. Upon her entry Henry rose to greet her.

'Come in, please sit down.' Henry spoke nervously.

She moved gracefully across the room and sat in the chair opposite us. The room fell so silent that I could hear the sound of her dress creasing as she took her seat.

Henry looked from her to me and back again. Finally he cleared his throat to speak.

'Forgive me, Rose, may I introduce Dora Mina.'

My eyes wandered over her as if studying a portrait in a gallery. Her fair skin and pale-blue eyes stood out against the backdrop of her raven-black hair. Her form was slight but not frail, and there was nothing about her I could observe that appeared rough or unpleasant. She was beautiful.

'My understanding is that you have come to speak with me. While I do not feel there is anything to be said between us I have agreed to receive you nonetheless.'

'I think you will find there is much I have to say that you would wish to hear, but I would like to speak with you privately, if Henry will allow it, that is.' She looked at Henry and gave him a gentle smile. My teeth sharpened.

Henry took hold of my hand and gently squeezed it. 'I shall leave the two of you alone, but will not be far off. Call me if you need me.' He stood and gave me a gentle kiss on the top of my head. I smiled. Even in her presence he was not afraid to show his devotion to me.

When Henry had left the room I addressed her. 'So what do you wish to say that could not be spoken freely in the presence of your fiancé?'

At first she did not answer me. Her gaze lowered from my eyes down to her hands.

'Pardon me, I seem suddenly to be at a loss for words. It is just that you are not at all as I imagined you to be. You are so young, so very beautiful. It is easy to see why Henry has become so enamoured of you.'

'That is very kind of you. In the spirit of honesty I should say that my mind's image of you was equally unjust.'

There was a gentle knock at the door and one of the maids entered carrying a silver tea tray. She poured us each of us a cup and excused herself.

'Where were we?' I asked. Putting the teacup to my lips I took a small sip; I savoured the taste. It had been so long since I had tasted anything other than blood.

'You can imagine my upset in learning of Henry's desire to call off our engagement. Of course I had suspected his devotion to me was waning, and when he left London so suddenly last month, there was much talk among our social circle. I was beside myself.' She picked her cup off the table and rested in on her lap. 'I cannot change events which have already occurred, but I have come to ask that you no longer see him.'

'I see. Well, Henry is free to do as he pleases. And it just so happens that for the moment I am what pleases him.' I was beginning to lose my patience with her.

'True as that may be, I believe that, if it were only he and I again, he could forget you and he could care for me once more, possibly even love me.' Her voice was strong and full of passion.

'Are you so certain that he ever truly cared for you? Was it not his father's will that he ask for your hand, rather than his own?'

'He may not have cared for me at first, but I believe his heart grew fond of me. He seems different now – changed somehow.'

'Perhaps you never really knew him, perhaps no one really does.' I put my empty cup back on the tray and leaned back into the settee.

'And you claim to know him better? You hardly know him at all!' she snapped.

'I know him better than most. The Henry you think you know does not exist. With you he is but a shadow of himself, a contrived persona cleverly crafted over years of encumbering expectations.'

Dora placed her cup down on the table. It rattled against its saucer as she did so. 'My words are lost on you and I fear no amount of reasoning will persuade you to give him up.' She stood. 'Do not be fooled into thinking you are more than a fleeting fancy. With time all boys lose interest in their most cherished playthings.' Turning from me in a whirl of purple taffeta she was gone.

Henry returned a moment later. 'I have just seen Dora out. She appeared rather shaken.'

'Yes, I fear she worked herself into a bit of a state. It was not my doing.' Henry did not say so, but I could tell he was worried I might have done something to upset her.

'What was discussed? Did she give any indication of her intentions?'

'She asked me to give you up, to leave you. She thinks she is in love with you; she may very well be.'

Henry looked disappointed; I could tell he had hoped that everything had been resolved. 'I see. Rose, I have given her no cause to think I am in love with her. She knows the nature of our betrothal; I have been affectionate towards her, yes, but I would not go as far to say that I have given her reason to love me.' He sat down beside me and took my hands in his. 'She will never understand what we have, how much you mean to me. To think that I could ever willingly give you up – such is the thinking of a young and simple girl who has no understanding of what a tumultuous force love is.' Henry sighed. 'I should have known she would not concede so easily. I should have never let her speak with you. It was not worth the upset it has caused.'

'I am not upset my love. You were hopeful and cannot be blamed for wishing all could be resolved. Let us put the issue to rest for the evening for I have grown weary of it. Tomorrow we will speak more on it; whatever happens we will find a way to be together, of that I am certain.' I tilted my head towards him and kissed him. My lips lingered on his for longer than usual, savouring his sweetness.

Sometime after midnight we undressed and climbed into bed together. Neither of us spoke a word, as I curled up into him and let him hold me while we both drifted off to sleep.

CHAPTER 11

As I run, the moss felt cool and damp beneath my bare feet. Tall trees surround me; I am weaving through them, away from something – someone. Through the trees I can now hear the echo of her voice. She is calling to me, her voice familiar and soothing, lulling me towards her. I run faster.

As I enter the clearing a girl appears before me as if from nowhere. Her long raven-black hair cascades down over her pale opulent skin, her golden eyes fixed on mine. Exposing her two elongated canine teeth her mouth stretches into a grin, red blood trickling down her face.

I can hear her voice, but her lips do not move. 'Come to me, my child. I have returned for you. You are alone no longer.' Her hand is now extended towards me. I reach out to touch her but, as my fingers entwine with hers, she vanishes…

Henry's hand on my shoulder pulls me from my dream. Without opening my eyes I turned to face him, to seek comfort in his presence, to nuzzle into his warmth – only he is not warm; he is cool, like me.

'I had nearly forgotten how beautiful you are, Rose, especially while sleeping.'

My eyes adjusted to the darkness. Beside me lay Oliver Weir. He was stretched across the spot normally occupied by Henry, his head propped up on his hand in a contented manner. I must still be dreaming.

'I am no dream, Rose.' His free arm was now wrapped securely around my waist, pulling me near. I could feel his strength, his differentness. 'Part of me wants you dead for what you did to me, but in this moment I cannot decide if I want to kiss you or kill you.' He pressed his lips hard against mine, pinning me down under his weight.

'Get off of me!' Now it was I who had him pinned. 'You should be dead.'

He laughed. 'You are very strong now, my little Rose. I suppose I will have to get used to that.'

Where is Henry? It was not yet daylight but I could not feel him near. 'God help you if you have harmed Henry in any way...' I threatened.

'Shh, Henry's fine. He left a short while ago by carriage; I came unnoticed.' Through the darkness his amber eyes shone. He was different now. The blackness was gone, his heart still. His skin felt smooth and cool beneath my hands.

'You are changed. How did this come to be?'

'It was your doing, my love. Your blood-stained tears sparked new life within my dying body. Poetic really, don't you think?' He pushed against me. For once there was no ambiguity between us. As his maker I could sense every emotion that coursed through him, every intention.

Moving quickly off of him I sat on the nearby settee. As the billowing bed-curtains settled Oliver crept forward and pulled them aside, so that there was an unobstructed view between him and me.

'You, too, are much changed, Rose. Gone is the timid little girl I once knew. Before me I see woman, strong and defiant.'

'Much has changed for the both of us, I suppose. Why have you come, why now?' I leaned back into the arm of the settee.

'I have been watching you for months, Rose. Watching as you moved from one companion to the next, whoring yourself out so you could play the part of a lady pretending to be human.' He smirked, as if the idea pleased him. 'You always did have a weakness for nice things.'

'I had no idea you were still alive, Oliver. Why risk exposing yourself? Surely if you wished me dead it would be better that I were not anticipating it.'

'Yes, I did take that into consideration, but I was too curious to stay away. I needed to know why you had taken such a liking for this lord of yours. What does he have that I do not?'

'He is none of your concern, Oliver. You have no claim over me. I am under no obligation to provide you with an explanation.' I was growing impatient. He needed to leave before Henry returned. If he found us together, I could only imagine what he would think.

Oliver was now sitting beside me. Leaning his head towards my neck he inhaled. 'I can smell him all over you. You reek of his humanity.' His hand caressed my knee and began to glide upwards.

'You would be wise to keep your hands to yourself,' I snapped, grabbing his hand.

'Why is it that you affect me so, even now, after everything? My desire for you is like an unquenchable thirst. I have tried to forget you, but no matter how many lives I drained, how many copper-haired women I bed, I could not put you out of my mind.' His mouth was eagerly searching mine, his hands grasping at the thin layer of fabric that separated my flesh from his. 'I want you more than I have ever wanted anything. From the first moment I laid eyes on you, I knew I had to possess you. But I fear it is now you who possesses me.'

His searching lips pressed against me, and this time I did not pull away. I wanted to stop him – I knew this time I could – but instead I found my lips receiving his and my body moving in response to his touch. I closed my eyes and leaned my head back as he kissed my neck. I felt the tips of his fangs graze my flesh. My mind was spinning, why was I not stopping him?

As his teeth ripped through my flesh I felt him enter me. The sensation was electrifying, as if my whole body was alight. As he moved within me the sense of my treachery grew. How could I have succumbed to such a loathsome man? He had finally got what he wanted and this time I was a willing participant.

Grabbing the back of my head he pulled my face forwards to look at him. I looked into his eyes and found my way back into the moment. Pressing my face against his I pulled him deeper, waves of pleasure came crashing over me, drowning me. When I could bear it no longer I screamed out in release.

Oliver collapsed on top of me. Kissing my exposed skin he rested his head upon my chest. 'I love you so much, Rose. I never stopped loving you.'

There was someone else in the room. Raising my head, I looked over the back of the settee and saw Henry standing in the open doorway.

'Henry!' I choked out, throwing Oliver off me on to the floor. He was quick to regain his footing and now stood staring intently at Henry.

'Leave us!' I shouted at Oliver. At the sight of Henry, I became gravely aware of what I had just done.

A satisfied grin stretched across Oliver's face. 'As you wish, Rose,' he said, brushing quickly past Henry as he left the room.

When I was certain Oliver had left the house, I turned to Henry. 'Henry please, it is not what you think.' My white nightshift was torn and stained with fresh blood. How could I explain if I could not deny?

'If he hurt you…' His gaze diverted from mine as if to spare me the shame.

Quickly I moved towards him and took his face in my hands. 'No Henry, but I must explain. I told you before of a man I knew, one who was cruel to me in a way no other has been. What I did not tell you was that I killed him.'

'Well, he is obviously not dead, Rose!'

'My actions are inexcusable but you must imagine the shock. This man, the man I killed, suddenly before me. I was confused. I made a mistake.'

Henry looked broken. Walking over to the bed he sat and placed his head in his hands. 'What power does he have over you that he can make your very will bend at the sight of him?'

'Henry, I wish I could explain. Perhaps it is because he is like me. The pull I felt towards him was so strong. I could not stop myself.' Approaching him I took his hands in mine. 'I know my actions are inexcusable, unforgivable. But my feelings towards you are unchanged. I still love you, Henry, with all of my heart.'

'You have no heart!' he yelled, his voice rising from deep within. 'You constantly use what you are as an excuse for your ill behaviour and I am tired of it. I have had enough!' He rose and headed towards the door. 'And to think I was willing to give up everything for you. My father was right: you are nothing more than a whore.'

'Henry, please, I never meant to hurt you.'

'After what he did to you – how could you do it? I just don't understand. I am not sure I ever will.' Henry now stood in the doorway, his back towards me. 'I care too much for you still to cast you out so close to the dawn, but come nightfall I want you gone from here. I never wish to see you again.'

His words stung. The weight of what I had done came crashing down. How could I have been so mindlessly hurtful? I began to weep. 'I am so sorry, Henry. Can you not find it in your heart to forgive me? You know what I am... You are my light, my goodness. Without you there is only darkness.'

'Perhaps if I had not seen... No, the image of you with him can never be erased from my mind. Like a weed it will spread, strangling all the love I ever had for you until there is nothing left.' With that he was gone.

I wanted to go after him but I was frozen with despair. Choking back my bloody sobs I willed death to come and take me away. He should have cast me out into the daylight, but that would have been too kind. Instead, I was left to suffer in the knowledge of what I had done, of what I had lost.

CHAPTER 12

When twilight finally came I gathered the strength to rise. I had not moved since Henry had walked out, leaving me alone in the room that had once been our sanctuary. Pouring some water from a jug into a small ceramic basin I washed away the dried blood from my face and hands. I slipped off my soiled shift and pulled on my garments from the day before. I focused my concentration on these small tasks, one thing at a time.

As I exited the room the house was silent; I could neither hear nor feel Henry present within its walls. Stepping out on to the street the cool air brushed cruelly against me. I needed to get as far away from there as my legs would take me.

If I stopped running, my grief would overcome me again and I would sink inside myself, sink inside the growing blackness. How could I have ever thought my happiness would last? This world had taken everything from me. Before Henry I had never known what my life was lacking. And although now, just as before we had ever met, I was alone, it was somehow different. There was a great sense of loss within me, as though something that had once occupied a part of me was missing.

As I ran forth through the blanket of fog, the sky opened up and rain began to fall. My pace slowed as I found myself on a familiar street – I was standing in front of an all-too-familiar door. Why had I come here?

The little brass lion on the glossy black door taunted me, as if daring me to knock.

'The house is long empty, Rose.' Oliver said, appearing as if from the shadows beside me. 'I had left the estate to you... As you could not be found my solicitor was instructed to seek out my wife and child.'

'Were they found?'

'The house remains unclaimed – they did not attend my funeral.'

'I'm sorry, Oliver. Perhaps they do not know... Perhaps they could not be found.'

'Perhaps they do not wish to be found.' Oliver said. There was a sadness in his voice, a loneliness.

'Your mother came... to pay her respects. She watched as they lay me in the ground.'

'I wish you would not speak of her. Like my father, she is dead to me.'

'And you to her. A headstone has been erected next to mine with your name on it, Rose.'

'I think I would like to see it. Will you take me there?'

Oliver nodded. We turned our back on the house that had played such a pivotal role in both of our fates.

In silence we walked; the city thinned and shrank behind us as we climbed up over the Heath. Several houses were still illuminated by the warm glow of candlelight; they seemed to dance in the darkness. Finally we ascended a long narrow road and came to a halt in front of the gates of Highgate Cemetery.

'Come,' Oliver said, taking my hand and leading me through the creaking iron gates.

Nocturnal creatures scurried around us; all else was silent. No one roused from their eternal slumber to greet us. We were alone.

Oliver and I now stood in front of a row of headstones, the graves covered with plain stone slabs.

'This is where I was laid to rest and there beside me, that's you.'

I looked down upon my gravestone: *Kirstin Rose Elizabeth Maines 1871–1887*. A single rose in partial bloom was carved into the stone – a life cut short. I would always be the age I was when I entered that forest that night. The night I died.

Oliver stood behind me, slipping his arms under mine and wrapping them around my waist. 'We are forever joined, Rose, tied by blood.' He leaned his face into my neck. I could feel the sharp tips of his fangs against my skin.

'Please don't. What happened before was a mistake.'

'A mistake you seemed to rather enjoy.' His arms tightened around my waist.

'My heart belongs to Henry – what I did to him was unforgivable. I will never forgive myself for hurting him.'

'But yet you forgive yourself for what you did to me?'

'I wanted you dead, wanted you to suffer for what you did to me.'

'What I did to you? Rose, I loved you. I may have been a bit cruel at times, I admit that, but what you did to me…'

Spinning around I met his gaze and held it. 'Cruel? Do you honestly not recall what you did to me – what you almost…'

His eyes searched mine. 'I was upset, drunk – I didn't know what I was doing, Rose. After you ran off I was beside myself with guilt for what I had done to you. But you drove me so crazy, I was out of my mind with want of you!'

'Is that why you have returned, why you could not simply leave me be? You have ruined everything!' The palm of my hand stung as it met Oliver's cheek.

I was flung backwards, crashing into a headstone. The stone cracked under the violence of the impact.

'You try my patience, Rose.'

'And you try mine!' I ran towards him and now had my hand around his neck, pressing him against the trunk of a nearby tree. 'You have stolen everything from me. You have tainted my love – the only thing left that was pure and good in this dark horrible existence.'

'Do not be so melodramatic.' Oliver removed my hand from around his throat. 'Are you so certain he even loved you? Men like him are different from us, Rose. They do not understand the weight we of less privilege bear, the struggles we have endured. Everything comes so easily to them. How are you so certain that you were ever anything more to him than a kept whore?'

'Only someone who had never truly known what it is like to be in love could think that. I know he loved me – he loves me still.'

'He will never be yours again. A man like that is too proud to recover from such betrayal.' His soiled hands worked at gathering up the fabric of my dress.

'You would be wise to remove your hands, Oliver, before I rip them off.'

He began to laugh. 'Still as stubborn as ever.' Removing his hands, he continued. 'Do not forget that we are bound. I can feel your hunger, your desire for me. You will not be able to resist me forever.'

'You know nothing of my impulses or my desires. I desire for only one person and that is Henry. His love has provided more nourishment than the blood of a thousand corpses. Without his love I shall starve, wither away into nothingness.' I began to sob, my heart full of pain.

'Why can you not love me, Rose? Are we so greatly different he and I. Am I still so repulsive to you even now?'

'I will never love you. I cannot.' In that moment I needed nothing more than to be away from that place, to be away from him. And so I was gone. I merely thought of fleeing and the action commenced. I was beginning to have a far greater control over my powers.

The house was dim but I could make out a soft orange glow coming from Henry's room. Scaling the facade I pulled myself up over the small balcony of his window. The curtain was only ever so slightly open, but it was enough for me to make out Henry's figure seated in front of the fire.

I entered through the window in one swift motion and was now standing before Henry.

'Why have you come, Rose? I meant what I said about not wishing to ever see you again.'

'I know you did, Henry, and I accept that. After this night you shall never lay eyes on me again, unless you wish it so. All you need do is call for me, and I will come.'

'Call for you?'

My urge to see him that night had come from outside of me, like some invisible force pulling me. 'We have exchanged blood. I think that makes us connected to one another somehow. I can sense you, feel you, even when you are not near. Did you not wish me here tonight?'

'You have consumed my thoughts ever since I first laid eyes on you. Why have you bewitched me so? I fear you have compelled me to love you and even if I will it I cannot put you out of my head.'

'Your words injure me, Henry. They are as a knife cutting away at my heart. My love for you is honest and pure. I have never had one ill-intention towards you. I may be a monster, but somehow with you I came to be more human than I had ever been before.' Kneeling before him I took his hand and placed it over my heart. 'You breathed life into my cold dead heart and I felt it beat – it beat with your blood; and now that warmth is fading, that life is spilling from my veins each moment I am separated from you.'

'Rose, please, I cannot bear to hear these words. You have broken my heart. I am not certain it shall ever mend.'

We sat for a moment in silence. He looked down, his eyes avoiding mine. 'You should go now.' He removed his hand from my chest and stood.

'Are there no more words to say?' I asked woefully.

'I do not believe there are,' Henry replied, walking towards the open window.

There was nothing I could say to heal the wound I had inflicted upon his heart. As I approached the window I leaned in to give him one last kiss. 'Goodbye my love,' I said as I pressed my lips to his. His lips received mine wilfully, his arms wrapped around my waist pulling me tight.

He lifted one hand and combed it through my hair, caressing me softly, and then clutching the back of my head he pulled me towards him and kissed me forcefully. I knew this was goodbye but I needed to feel him close to me one last time, to savour his warmth, his scent. As he lowered me to the ground I tore away at the layers of fabric that formed a barrier between us.

We made love in front of the warm glow of the fire, and although it was gentle and sweet I could tell the moments when he remembered what I had done to him. I wanted to make him forget, to wipe the memory from his mind. But I would not do so without his permission. As he quickened his tempo my hunger began to take over. I could feel my urge to feed rising from within.

Looking into my eyes he covered my mouth with his hand. He was punishing me; he wanted me to suffer the denial. He did not remove his eyes from mine as he took his final thrusts before collapsing on top of me. Between heavy breaths he spoke: 'I am marrying Dora Mina. The wedding is in two weeks.' He rolled off of me, sprawling out beside me.

I could feel the moisture begin to pool in my eyes and as I shut them tight I could feel the crimson liquid spill over.

Henry leaned over and kissed my eyes, clearing away the streams of tears with his hand. 'Farewell, my dark angel.'

I rose and walked towards the open window. The curtains billowed in the cool nocturnal breeze. 'If you should ever need me all you have to do is call my name and I will come.'

With those words I leaped from the window into the still night. As I walked away from the house I turned and saw Henry standing in his window. A moment later he drew the curtain and was gone.

CHAPTER 13

When I left Henry that night I felt empty and lost. I needed to go to ground for a while and be still, to re-evaluate my role in life and what I was to do next. I found myself back at Highgate Cemetery – I lay down within my very own tomb and pulled the stone slab over me, shutting out the vibrant glow of the approaching dawn.

I am not certain how many nights I lay there undisturbed in the ground. I had moments of consciousness, which I assumed occurred each evening but could not say for certain. I grew very weak and my powers diminished. You must understand – I was not trying to kill myself, I was simply trying to be still for a while. My life had taken such drastically unimaginable turns over the past year that I could not bear to make another decision until I could come to terms with what I had become and all that had happened to me.

I was a child of the night, a vampire. I had been so since that awful night when I fled from Mr Weir into that forest. Why had I been chosen for such a fate? What purpose had it served? I wanted so much to be good, to be proper. I had managed to escape the clutches of Mr Weir that night when he had tried to force himself on me, to steal my innocence – and for what? What had I truly been spared? By fleeing, had I not suffered a greater assault on my purity? Was my soul not damned?

The only innocence I had left, the only morsel of purity, I had given over to Henry; and now he too was gone. How had I been so naive to think I could turn my back on my own wickedness, that I could somehow be redeemed through a life of sin with Henry? I had given my whole self to him. The last drop of humanity I had left I fed to him on a gilded spoon and he had spat it back in my face.

I could feel the anger building inside of me, stirring from within. Why had I been such a fool? Henry had treated me like his whore and then expected me to be his pure and innocent possession, just as Oliver had. I resolved that no man would ever have so much power over me again.

With the little force that remained to me I lift the stone covering of my grave. The moonlight shown down upon me, illuminating my pale white skin as I propelled myself forward out of the cemetery and down towards the Heath. I needed to feed.

In no time at all I located a deer and a few pheasants to feed on. But my hunger was not yet satisfied and I thirsted for human blood.

Bathing first in one of the Heath's ponds, ridding myself of blood and soil, I made my way towards the East End.

I had no trouble at all locating the whorehouse Henry had brought me to previously. I lifted my hand to the red door and gave a quick hard knock. After a brief moment, the madam opened the door and looked down at me. 'Not with yer gentleman this evening?'

'No, Ma'am. I am alone and in need of lodgings.' I looked up at the madam from under my copper mess of curls.

'As fetching as you may be, sweet one, this is not a guesthouse and I have no use for another used-up plaything. You best be on yer way, luv.' She began to shut the door.

'I assure you, my virtue is intact, Ma'am.' I could see that this had grabbed her attention for she closed the door no further but instead inspected me more carefully with her pale-grey eyes.

'Hurry inside then and let me take a better look at ya.' She took me by the arm and near dragged me over the threshold.

Now inside I surveyed the occupants. The house was relatively empty. 'Slow night?'

'Humph – I suppose it is. What's it to you then?'

'Well, I suppose that means your rooms are not all occupied at the moment. Surely you have room to accommodate me for one night?'

'You stay, you work – them's the rules. I ain't making no exceptions.'

'Very well, show me to my lodgings.'

The madam led me upstairs to one of the vacant rooms. Once inside she advised me to clean up, put my face on and put on something decent. I suppose I must have looked like something that had crawled out of the ground, and I smelled of pond water to boot.

A few hours later there was a knock at the door. 'Rose, I have a gentleman caller to see you.'

She led him inside and left us alone. 'Rose, is it?' he asked, removing his jacket and placing it over the back of the chair.

I nodded. 'And what shall I call you?'

He sat down. 'You may call me Halden.' He began to unbutton his waistcoat. 'I would like you to remove your clothing.'

Unfastening my garments I let them drop to the floor.

'Now, sit on the bed,' he instructed. He finished undressing and walked towards me. 'You are very beautiful. I will enjoy having you.'

I observed his naked form. He was not unpleasant to look at, but it was not his body I wanted, it was his blood. 'Lie back,' he ordered sharply, and as I did as he asked he climbed on to the bed and rested his body on top of mine.

My teeth sharpened at the scent of him, the feeling of his warm skin against mine. I could feed on him and be done with him, but part of me needed to succumb, wanted to succumb. As if I was seeking retribution, a way to cleanse myself of any goodness that remained.

As he entered me I cried out. He was not gentle with me – I was his whore. I was his, bought and paid for, and he would be sure to get his money's worth.

When it was over he lay beside me. I felt numb. For the first time since the change I felt truly dead. Climbing on top of him I pinned his hands above his head.

'I am not quite ready to go again, pet. But I admire your eagerness to please me,' he chuckled breathlessly.

'It is not your pleasure I seek but my own.' Exposing my fangs I caught a glimpse of the horror that came across his face before I buried my fangs into his neck. He struggled, but I was too strong for him. I felt my body returning to life as I drained the liquid from his veins.

When I was finished I lifted myself off of him. He stared up at me, his expression frozen, unchanging. He was dead. I rolled his body into a dusty tattered rug and carried him down to the banks of the Thames. I had killed him and I felt no shame. I had no one left to answer to for my actions. I could compel anyone I wanted to forget they had seen me. There was no one to judge me – I was free.

CHAPTER 14

Over the next couple of days I made arrangements to leave London for Paris. I could no longer bear the familiarity of the city that had stolen so much from me.

Slipping away from the port at Dover I thought I saw Oliver watching me depart from the shore. Had he waved farewell? It was only a matter of time before he would seek me out again. Even in death he was determined to make me his.

As we made passage over the Channel that night, I felt the last morsel of my humanity slipping away. Henry had brought me back from such a dark place; he had resurrected me as Jesus had raised Lazarus from the dead. Without him I felt the light slipping away. But I could not return, I feared what I was capable of doing if I stayed; of what I might do to make him mine again. He was better off without me. At least now he would have a chance at a normal life, he and Dora could be happy.

Closing my eyes, I inhaled the sea air and let the memory of his face slip away.

Paris was a dream – a wild, vivid, manic dream full of wonderment and life. I felt awake for the first time in as long as I could remember. Free from the thick veil of London's fog-bound atmosphere my head felt clear.

I found my place amongst the entertainers of the cabarets and music halls. Having never had many female companions, I adjusted to their constant company. These beautiful creatures of the underground were different from any women I had known; they were electric, liberated and strong. They treated me like a sister, affectionately calling me *la jolie petite Rose*; I was loved.

They each had their own unique talents and I received a first-class education in the seduction and pleasure of men. I was an empty vessel and they filled me to the brim with their knowledge. But it was still a man's world and as women our job was to entertain them.

Drowning myself in the excesses of Parisian nightlife, I had my fill of absinthe-soaked gentlemen. I tried to forget Henry, but each dawn as I closed my eyes to the breaking day, it was his face I saw, his voice that called out to me. No matter whose arms I lay entwined within, it was his sweet embrace I longed for.

Months had passed and I had still not forgotten him. Even though I vowed not to contact him, I felt the need to put pen to paper and try and expel the unbearable grief at long last.

My dearest Henry,

I hope that this letter finds you and that you are not still so pained that you will destroy it before reading its contents. I do not seek your forgiveness, I have no right to. For the pain I have caused you I cannot even forgive myself.

These words I write to you in a selfish attempt to unburden myself to you; to salvage any goodness that remains in me, however slight.

Perhaps it will do some good to remind you that I have only just turned ten and six and therefore I lack the wisdom that your sex, age and station in life affords you. While I do not consider myself a silly girl, I was never educated in the ways of men. As you know, my father died when I was a young girl and my mother hardly paid heed to me when I began to attain womanhood.

I believe Mr Weir – whom you met ever so briefly, and under the most unfortunate circumstances – recognised this innocence in me when we first met. His intent, although not known to me at first, was to make me his possession. He toyed with my affections in such a manner that I often felt dizzy and confused. He was violent and cruel towards me. At times I feared what might become of me.

After a failed attempt to rob me of my virtue I fled. That was the night I was 'turned'. It will not surprise you to learn that his was the first life I took. And I am not ashamed to admit that it gave me great pleasure to watch his life drain from him.

You can imagine my surprise and disbelief when I saw him before me again, very much alive. But of course he was not alive: like me he was living dead, a vampire. Like two savage beasts we were drawn to one another.

I have often denied my feelings towards Mr Weir — but even though I despised him and found him most vile, I secretly took pleasure in his affections. He was the first man to ever dote on me.

Admittedly, I am guilty of all you have accused me of. I only wish to explain that what happened between Oliver and me had nothing to do with love. I can no longer use what I have become as an excuse for my actions, but you must understand that at times I am like a feral animal that, when caged for too long, begins to nip at the ankles of its master.

I hope that you have found happiness with Dora Mina. You deserve the love of a lady as proper and uncomplicated as she. She is simple. She is good.

One day your heart may soften enough to forgive me for my betrayal. I shall keep my distance from London until I can fully trust that I will not try to see you or interfere in your affairs.

The hours I spent with you were the happiest of my life. My blackened heart belongs to you and you alone. You will forever be my always.

Eternally yours,

Rose.

I arranged to have the letter posted the next day. I did not give a return address.

CHAPTER 15

The first time I noticed her, she was standing amongst the crowd at the Moulin Rouge. It was just a fleeting exchange, her amber eyes fixed on mine and in a whirl of raven-black hair she was gone.

Three nights later I saw her again, this time she lingered a little bit longer, enough for me to make out her pale childlike face, but again she disappeared before I could approach her. She continued to appear over the next two weeks, much in the same fashion, sometimes following as I went on my nightly walk around Montmartre in search of a meal.

Finally one cool night in November she decided it was time to make her presence known to me.

Aware she was following me, I had turned into Montmartre Cemetery. We would not be disturbed here; the slumbering occupants would not stir.

'Who are you?' I turned to face my stalker and was surprised that she was suddenly standing so near.

'You do not recognise me?'

I studied her pale face. Her glowing amber eyes shone in the darkness and the blackness of her hair seemed to disappear into the darkness of the night. 'Of course, that night in the forest – you attacked me!' I felt my breath quicken at the memory.

'Attacked? No, I transformed you.'

'You murdered me!'

'I liberated you, gave you a new life, a better one.'

My head was spinning. Why now? Why had she come to me?

As if reading my thoughts she answered me. 'You have wandered astray from your path, Rose. It is my fault – I should have come to you sooner, but there were reasons I could not.'

My legs felt weak. Sitting down on one of the graves I attempted to regain my composure. 'I do not understand.' I shook my head in disbelief. 'You left me for dead.'

'Death is part of the process of rebirth, my child. Your mortal life must be lost in order to rise again.'

'You left me – I was all alone. I woke up confused, terrified … changed. I knew not what I was, what I was capable of.' The memory of that first awakening came rushing back to me. I had never been so scared in all my life, had never felt so alone.

'But you are not alone – you have never been alone.'

'Why? Why me? And the dreams… It was as if I knew all along what would happen.'

She stepped towards me, placing her hand upon my shoulder. 'This was your destiny, Rose. The dreams served as a guide, to lead you to us.'

'Us?'

'There are more than just you and I, Rose. I have lived many lifetimes, as will you. At times I have felt it necessary to create another. I felt the call, if you will. You have many sisters, Rose, the chosen ones. One day you shall meet them – when you are ready. When I can be assured of their safety.'

How old was she? She looked not much older than I, but how many years had she remained the same? How many decades, centuries even, had passed?

'You seek answers, but now is not the time for questions.'

'What good are you to me, then, if you offer me no answers? I do not even know your name!'

'You may call me Lily. But please there are some things that must be dealt with rather urgently. Once they are taken care of you may ask me whatever you like.'

'What has any of this to do with me?' I asked.

'Your child Weir draws too much attention through his careless behaviour. He puts us all at risk.'

'He is none of my concern. I care not what he does'

'He is your responsibility. You must return to London and take control of the situation. If you do not, we will be forced to take action.' Lily's face had hardened, no longer smooth and angelic-looking.

'Do with him as you wish. I care not what becomes of him.'

'You are connected through blood, you are his maker. You cannot imagine the pain felt when one of our children meets the final death.'

'How can you destroy him? I thought we were immortal.'

'We have limitations. All that we are, our essence, our dark soul, must have a vessel. Our body is our keeper – if it is destroyed beyond regeneration, we perish. Decapitation, prolonged exposure to sunlight, irreparable damage to the heart such as its removal... these are fatal.'

For a brief moment I thought of ripping out her heart and setting it alight.

Her hand pressed against my chest. 'You have no idea how much stronger I am than you, how much quicker!'

I closed my eyes. Would it be so awful ... to die – to die again?

Her hand dropped. 'You must trust that I only want what is best for our kind, to protect us. You cannot possibly understand the great risk you have brought to us, to your sisters?'

'Surely it is Oliver who is to blame, not I?'

'No, Rose, I speak not of him. He will be dealt with one way or another. There are those who seek to destroy us. If they learn of Henry's knowledge of our kind, they will destroy him. You will be held accountable for revealing your nature to a mortal and I will be blamed for allowing you to do so. We are all in danger. I am giving you a chance to save him, to save us before it is too late.'

'He would not be in danger had you explained all this to me sooner!'

'What's done is done. You must go to him and erase all knowledge of what you are. He must forget you ever existed.'

'And if I refuse?'

'Then I shall. Would you not like the opportunity to say farewell? You can take away his pain, Rose, his suffering. You will be doing him a favour.'

'A favour! Although he may not remember the love we shared, he will feel the loss of it. There will forever be a void where it once resided.'

'Ever the romantic! How do you know he loves you still? Has he once tried to find you, written to you? He turned his back on you, forgot you and married another. But yet you fight so hard to hold on to him?'

'I betrayed him, I broke his heart. But I believe one day he will forgive me. He has to forgive me.'

'To him you were nothing more than a temporary distraction from his obligations.'

'You have no idea what we had, what we were to one another.' My eyes began to swell with moisture.

'Give him up – he is yours no longer. He belongs to another now; let him live his life in peace. If you do as I ask, everything will be as it should.'

'You do not ask, you order!'

'And what of it? You would be wise to argue no further. My patience wanes, Rose.'

'Is it not enough that you have robbed me of my life, that you now seek to take away the only joy I have left?'

'I have not willed him to turn his back on your love, Rose. This was all your doing. You seek forgiveness yet refuse to be held accountable for your actions. What are you holding on to, Rose? Do you really think he could ever forget, ever forgive? Do you think he will ever look on you the same way again?'

Her words cut into my heart like a knife. Perhaps she was right. What claim did I have to him now? Did he not deserve a chance at happiness? Had I been so blind, so selfish, not to see what he had been willing to give up for me – and I threw it all away?

'One day you will understand why you have suffered, why it has been necessary. You belong with your sisters; you will see how different things can be. Once you have erased all memory Henry has of you and resolved things with Oliver I will come for you.'

She turned and began to walk away. Her long slender shadow stretched across the graves in the moonlight. 'Oh … and, Rose, if you disobey me, I will kill them. I cannot have us put in danger by a pair of *men*.' Her emphasis on their sex made me wonder – why sisters and not brothers? Why only girls?

As she disappeared through the gate I let out the tears I had been forcing back. The thought of losing Henry forever tipped me over the edge. I could not bear the thought of it. What was I to do? If I did not do as she asked, she would kill him. Of what … whom was she so scared? The thought of someone, something, intimidating her – this was not someone I ever wished to encounter.

Standing alone amongst my fellow dead, I envied their stillness, their peace. No one would ask anything of them ever again – they were free.

CHAPTER 16

Over the next couple of days I made arrangements for my return to London and said my farewells to my companions. I would miss my little family of misfits dearly. With them I had found solace, a place to fit in among those who lived on the edges, within the shadows.

I knew in my heart that I would one day return to Paris but whether it would be months, years or even decades from now I could not say. I could not predict what would happen next, what Lily had in store for me. Nothing made sense to me. But does any child understand the will of their elders?

As I approached London, I could feel the pull of Henry stronger than ever. I wondered how long it would take to no longer feel tied to him; would I feel the severance?

I needed to mentally prepare myself; I was not quite ready to part with him. I would go to Oliver first.

Before Oliver had made himself known to me that unfortunate night at Henry's, there had been an unexplainable cloudiness in my mind, like a memory you try to recall but cannot fully grasp. It was not until I learned of his resurrection that the fog began to clear. Now that I was back in London I could sense him clearly, could feel his mood. I knew where I could find him.

As I made my way through the streets of London the city somehow felt different, as if it recalled everything that occurred under the lamplight, beneath the fog, forever growing, forever changing. It was a living organism and I was just one of many parasites taking refuge within it.

I soon found myself standing beneath the familiar glow of a

red lamp. I should have guessed this is where I would find him.

Rapping loudly I waited to be invited in. The door flung open and the madame stood towering over me, filling the void which was only a moment ago a closed entry. 'You again – what do ya' want this time?' she asked perturbed.

'I want you to take me to Oliver Weir.'

'You caused enough trouble last time you were 'ere, luv. You best be going before I have ya removed.'

I took a step up and looked her in the eyes. 'You will take me to see Mr Weir now.'

The stern lines around her mouth began to soften. 'Well, come in then, don't be loitering on my doorstep.'

Once inside she led me up the staircase to the third landing and stopped before one of the doors. She turned to me with a look of bewilderment, as if she could not quite recall what she was doing there.

'Well, go on then – knock,' I instructed and without another moment of hesitation she did just that.

I could hear the sound of laugher from within the room. 'Who is it?' Oliver called out playfully. 'If it's the devil come to collect, tell him I'm not quite ready to receive him.' There was another outburst of laughter. He was certainly in a merry mood this evening.

'Hand me your key and step aside,' I ordered the madam. She pulled a long metal chain out from her bosom and handed it to me – the master key.

Sliding the key into the lock I turned and swung the door slowly open. I hung the key back around the madame's neck. 'Now leave us, and take your little whores with you.'

'Come on, girls – Oliver here has a visitor,' she called to the women inside the room.

Oliver was seated in a dingy green-velvet armchair. His black hair was dishevelled and wild. His white shirt was open, revealing his pale bare chest; over it he wore a charcoal-grey waistcoat that also hung open. In his hand he held a half-drunk bottle of whisky. The look suited him somehow and was strangely appealing as if more true to his character than his usual clean-cut attire.

The girls pushed by me and I closed the door behind them. I removed my hat and cloak and draped them over the chair opposite Oliver and sat down.

He took a long swig from his bottle. 'Well, this is a surprise. I honestly wondered if I would ever see you again.'

'And yet here I am. We have both made mistakes, Oliver – I have come to set things right between us. A conversation is long overdue, do you not agree?'

'Oh I most certainly agree,' he smirked. 'We are so much alike Rose – yet you sit before me as superior and self-righteous as ever.'

His amber eyes locked on to mine. I missed their blackness. He was right: after all that had passed between us, how could I still think myself better than he. Had he not paid for his ill-behaviour with his very life? He was no more responsible for what had passed between Henry and me than I was. I had made a choice, a choice to betray him. If anyone else was to blame for all that had happened, it was Lily. Was she not at the very root of everything?

'I forgive you, Oliver. We have both done wrong by each other, and I cannot hold you responsible for everything that has gone awry in my life. Willed it or no, I am eternally bound to you.'

Oliver took another swig, this time draining the bottle. 'Well, well, little Rose has at last forgiven me.' He stood and stumbled towards me, though with his quick ability to correct his movements it was more like a jittery blur. He placed one hand on either arm of my chair.

'Now will you stop behaving so irresponsibly?' I asked.

'Irresponsibly – Ha! I have done nothing that you yourself have not also done.'

'I have made mistakes, I admit that. But I am not the one leaving bodies all over the streets of London. It is careless.'

'You really haven't changed much at all, Rose... Still so concerned about what others think.' He leaned into me and pressed his lips against mine.

I turned my head. 'I may have forgiven you, Oli, but my feelings towards you remain unchanged.'

He laughed and reached into his vest pocket, pulling out a gold cigarette case. He lit a cigarette and sat back down.

'New case?' I recalled the silver one he had used to carry with him.

'Ah yes, I liberated this from a gentleman the other night, I don't think he will miss it,' he grinned.

He took a drag of his cigarette and exhaled. 'So, you're still hung up on that Lord ... Henry – was that his name?'

'You know his name, and that is none of your concern,' I snapped.

'Touchy subject, I see. You did not really think they would let you keep him, did you?'

'You speak as though you know their minds.'

'I know enough to understand that your attachment to that mortal is a disgrace to your kind.'

'So you have spoken to them? What did they say?'

'We spoke only briefly, after you left me for dead; someone had to clean up your mess, to ensure my staff did not raise the alarm. When I woke up I was buried six feet underground. Lily resurrected me. She explained to me what I was, what I had become and that I must seek you out, that I must forgive you. I'm surprised she didn't leave me to rot, actually. She doesn't appear to be my biggest fan.' He stubbed out his cigarette on the table next to him. 'The truth is I owe you a debt of gratitude for liberating me from my dull mortal life, for the way things have panned out.'

'Of course, you would see it that way – you have sacrificed so little. In a way you have got everything you wanted.'

'Not everything,' he corrected, fixing his eyes on mine.

We sat in silence for some time. What more could we say that had not already been spoken? We had made our peace with one another. Where would we go from there? The thought of having him by my side for an eternity displeased me. But what other option did I have. Until he was able to better control his urges I would have to keep a watchful eye over him. If I did not, they would come and they would destroy him. Part of me wondered if that would really be so bad – would I really mourn the loss of him? It was not a decision I was prepared to make just yet. I needed time and I needed answers. But before any of that I needed to ensure Henry was out of harm's way.

'There is something I must attend to. I shall leave you in the company of your whores for a little while longer.'

'You will come back?' His words were full of longing – and desperation.

'Yes, Oliver, I will come back. But then we must leave this place, I think it taunts me – reminds me of a time I wish to forget.

'I know a place we can go. You will feel very much at home there.'

I stood and Oliver was suddenly behind me placing my cloak gently over my shoulders. His fingers grazed my neck. 'You are the only one for me, Rose. I will wait for you as long as it takes.'

I placed my hand over his and gave it a gentle squeeze. 'Your heart is wasted on me.'

'No, Rose, I do not believe it is. You may not be able to admit it even to yourself, but you care for me. I know you do.'

'You would be wise not to mistake my company for a sign of affection. I am simply following orders.'

'And what orders are those?'

'To either accept you as my child and keep a close watch over you, or to destroy you. I have not yet made up my mind as to which is the lesser burden to bear.'

CHAPTER 17

I stood outside of Henry's house on Grosvenor Square. The windows were dark but I could sense him within. Scaling the wall I entered through one of the windows.

Henry was fast asleep, his arms wrapped around Dora Mina's swollen belly; arms which had once belonged to me. I was not prepared for the effect seeing them together would have on me. I never wanted someone dead as much as I did her in that moment. I could feel the wetness spill from my eyes.

Henry stirred, his eyes slowly fluttered open. I moved to his side and placed my hand over his mouth. I did not want him to wake her.

He seemed to understand and cautiously he rose from the bed. Pulling on his discarded dressing gown and fetching a lamp he followed me out of the room. When we were safe inside the drawing room he broke the silence.

'Rose, what are you doing here?'

It seemed tonight was the night for playing the role of the unexpected caller.

'I know I promised to stay away and I had every intention of doing so. But the situation has changed.'

Henry sat down. 'You have no idea how much I have missed you, Rose. How many nights I have lain awake wishing only to look upon your face once more, to feel your touch. You must understand, Dora and I...'

'Shh, you need not explain. I have not come to interfere. She has been able to give you what I could not. What I wrote in my letter was true: I only wish for you to be happy. She can give you that whereas I bring only death and despair.'

'Then why have you come?'

'My selfishness has put you in danger. I was wrong in believing my love for you would not hold consequences.' I turned my back to him; I could feel the tears forming in my eyes once more.

Henry rose and stood behind me. 'Do not turn away from me, my love.' He turned me to face him and pressed his lips gently upon mine. I could taste my tears as they rolled between our lips.

'You must forget me,' I whispered, my eyes still closed. 'It must be as though we never met.' I opened my eyes and looked into his glistening blue eyes. It was time.

'No! I will not allow it!' He broke eye contact and abruptly turned away from me.

'I must! You are in mortal danger if I do not! They will come for you!'

'Who will come for me? You speak in riddles I do not understand. Explain to me why you seek now to erase all we have had.'

'I cannot! You know too much already. Please, allow me to take away the pain I have caused you, the heartache. I wish only to give you peace.' I pleaded with him, wrapping my arms around his waist and resting my head upon his back.

'Peace? There is no greater loss than that of love, Rose. Do you really think my heart will ever heal? Even if it does not recall whom it has loved, it will remember it has and it will forever mourn for the loss of it!'

'Henry, please,' I begged. 'They will come... They will kill you. I have no choice in the matter... It is beyond my control!'

'Then let them come. For I would rather die than to have never known you.' He placed his head in his hands; I could feel the trembling of his body as he began to weep.

'Do you not think I have not uttered these very words? I have begged and pleaded to not have to make this impossible choice. But I must. The decision has been made.' I hated Lily for making me do this. I understood so little of anything she did. What purpose could any of this possibly serve?

Someone else was in the room. I had not heard them approach. 'Henry, what is the meaning of this – why is she here?'

It was Dora. She stood in the now open doorway. Her hair hung loose around her shoulders and her round belly protruded from beneath her nightshift.

'Dora, what are you doing out of bed. You know what the doctor said, you must rest.' He went to her side and reached out for her.

She pulled away. 'Is that blood on your hands? Are you injured?'

Henry looked down; his hands were red with blood from my tears. 'I'm fine, Dora.'

'Why is she here? Haven't you caused us enough trouble?' Dora's legs gave way beneath her and she began to fall. I rushed to her side and caught her before she hit the ground.

Startled, she stared up at me. 'What creature is this who can move without being seen?'

Henry helped her up and placed her arm around his shoulder for support. 'You are delirious, love. Let's get you back to bed.'

'I know what I see: she has blood upon her face. She is a devil come to steal my baby! Send her away! Send her away!' She was hysterical. I looked at Henry. He nodded in approval to my silent request.

'Dora, look at me.' His eyes met mine, they were wide with fear. 'You had a bad dream, you dreamed Henry loved another, that he refused to marry you…'

'But this is true – it was you he loved. You tried to take him from me!'

'No, Dora, I did not. Henry loves you. It was a bad dream. In the morning you will wake and he will be lying beside you. You will remember your wedding day, the day you learned of your first child, his child, growing within you. You will smile and be filled with joy. Now let Henry take you to bed. You will not remember I was here. You have never looked upon my face – you do not know me.'

She blinked and seemed to look right through me. 'Henry, why am I away from bed? What is the hour? Please return me to our bed, for I must rest.'

Henry lifted her up into his arms and carried her from the room. He stopped at the stairs and called to me: 'Will you wait?'

'I will not go, not yet.'

I watched as he carried her up the staircase. He really did care for her, didn't he? I sat down and removed my hat, wiping my face clean on the edge of my cloak. I knew what I had to do; I had to let him go.

When Henry did not return I went to find him. I needed to finish what I had come to do. I could not risk putting him further in harm's way. I had felt someone following me, watching me since I had arrived back in London. Was it Lily come to ensure that I followed through on her commands?

As I climbed the stairs towards Henry's bedroom I sensed something was not right. Henry was in danger. I bolted into the room. Across the bed lay Dora bloodied and unmoving. She was curled into a ball, her hands around her belly.

I quickly scanned the room. Where was Henry? That is when I saw a long lanky figure standing before me. It was not Lily but another. She looked to have been the same age as me when she turned. Her long brown hair was soaked with blood plastered to her pale skin.

'Who are you?'

'I am Adah, Daughter of Lilith, sister of Rose.'

Where was Henry? I could not focus; I was so overwhelmed with fear and confusion. And then I saw him; he lay behind her on the floor unmoving, a pool of blood forming beneath the open wound in his neck.

'What have you done?'

I rushed towards him, but she caught me and threw me backwards, sending me crashing against the wall.

'I did what you would not. I was sent by our maker to follow you, to make certain you did what she asked.'

I ran towards Henry once more, and again was sent flying backwards. I was furious. I could not tell if Henry was still alive but I needed to try and help him. It was my fault. 'Let me help him! I was going to do it!'

I was sobbing uncontrollably. I crawled over to Dora and placed my hand against her neck. She was dead.

'What reason had you to kill the innocent mother of an unborn child? I had already erased all memory of me. She remembered me no more.'

'An unfortunate accident. She became hysterical when she saw me. I could not contain the situation. Your Henry got in the way, I am afraid. I did not come to harm him.'

'You lie! You have overpowered me twice and yet you pretend a frail sickly woman was no match for you!'

'It matters not: what is done is done.'

'Please, you must let me help him!' The words choked their way out between my sobs.

'I cannot. You love him too much to ever let him go.'

Henry gasped. He was still alive but he did not have long. I began to wail. My mind was overcome with grief. I could not lose him. This was all my fault.

'Compose yourself, child. You are Daughter of Lilith! Do not waste your tears on this mortal man.'

'Daughter of Lilith?' This was the second time she had referred to Lily as Lilith, but it had only now registered. 'As in the first wife of Adam?'

'But of course – do you not know what you are, who you are, who you are destined to be?'

'I know nothing!'

I was so angry, so tired of all the half-truths and lies, of all the talk of destiny and greater purpose. The anger swelled inside of me. Like a tidal wave it lifted me and propelled me forward. This time I did not try to reach Henry and instead leapt on top of her and began to claw at her face. She struggled but my fury empowered me and I was not so easily overcome. Still, I could feel her beginning to overpower me. I looked at Henry. He was still, his chest unmoving. I could no longer feel his presence.

The door came crashing down and Oliver came rushing in. He was covered in blood. He leapt upon Adah in a single powerful bound and the two of us began to overpower her, ripping at her flesh. She began to struggle less, her blood spilling from her open wounds.

'I've got her!' Oliver shouted. 'Go to him.'

I did not hesitate. I rushed to Henry's side and tore into my wrist, letting the blood flow from the open wound into his mouth. He did not move.

I looked up at Oliver. 'Rip her head off!'

He wrapped his arms around her neck and in one swift twist her head came clean off. I felt a sharp pang inside me, as if a piece of me had been torn away. Was it her death or Henry's I felt?

Oliver came to my side. 'Will he live?'

'I am too late. His heart stopped before I could get to him.'

'But you gave him your blood. Do you think he will rise again?'

I had made the error in assuming death once before, Oliver knew that all too well. 'We will take him with us. We will take him to Highgate and put him in the ground.'

'What do we do with her?' He looked towards Adah.

'Burn her, burn it all!' I said, not just because I knew it was the only way to ensure that Adah was truly gone, but because I wanted to be rid of this place once and for all. These walls which had once held so many good memories were now poisoned by memories of all that I had lost.

Oliver disappeared and returned a moment later with a lamp.

Its orange glow illuminated the ghastly scene before us. How had it come to this?

I lifted Henry into my arms and carried him from the room. A moment later I heard the sound of glass breaking and saw the glow of the flames beginning to rise.

The front door hung on its hinges. Oliver must have broken the door down. Why had the staff not raised the alarm? As I stepped over the body of one of the maids, I understood. Why had he come to my aid?

'Because I love you, Rose,' he said, responding to my unspoken question. 'Without you I am nothing.'

'Perhaps you really have changed, Oliver. I do not think the old you would have done so.'

'That is where you have always been wrong about me. Don't you know I would do anything for you, anything to make you happy?'

I thought back on all the times he had followed me home through the streets of London. How had I not seen it before? He was trying to keep me safe. For how many nights after he turned had he followed me?

'Every night, Rose, every night until Paris.' His words were soft and sincere. He really did love me.

'They will come for us now,' I said softly as if to myself. I was not naive enough to think Lilith would not seek retribution for my treachery. I knew there would be a price to pay for disobeying her, for Adah's final death.

'I believe they are already on their way. Let me go to them, to explain. It is I who must answer for her child's death, not you. You did everything she asked of you. If it was not for her interference…'

He did not have to speak the words. If it was not for her interference Henry would be alive. I looked down at his lifeless body in my arms. Would he wake?

'No, we will face them together.' I knew there would be no

redemption for us, no salvation, but we had to try. We owed it to ourselves to try.

The blaze grew higher behind us as we walked forward into the night; I could feel its warmth on my back. If I closed my eyes, I could almost feel the sun.

EPILOGUE

Frozen in slumber we lay entwined. The sun was dipping below the horizon for the third time since Henry and I had gone into the ground. If he was going to rise, it would be tonight.

I called to him softly through the unbearable silence. 'Henry, it's Rose. Wake up. Please, you must wake…' He did not stir. I could feel the emptiness filling the space inside me that he had once occupied.

The creatures of the night began to move above us, called forth by the moonlight. I felt weak; how long had it been since I fed? Not since Paris.

I tried to stifle the hunger. I could not leave him alone in the ground – I would lay and wait forever, even if he never woke again.

I let my mind wander in the darkness. I could sense the others. Oliver lay asleep in the grave beside us. Lilith would be here soon, and she was not alone.

'You need to wake – they are coming and they won't let me keep you. They will take me away from you. I beg of you, if you can hear me, please open your eyes.' I pressed my wet face against his, kissing him softly.

Suddenly two glowing blue eyes pierced the darkness. I felt the tearing of his teeth into my neck. I struggled to stop him, but within the confined space it was difficult. I was too weak.

'Stop! Stop!' I shouted.

I felt his teeth release my broken flesh. 'Rose?'

'Henry! Yes, it is I, my love. You are awake. I was not too late!' I covered him in desperate kisses.

Then, as if suddenly remembering the events of three days before, he stopped me.

'Dora? My child?'

'Oh, Henry, I am so sorry. I did not come in time…'

Henry began to cry. 'I could not save them – she was so strong,' he recollected.

'Shh, there was nothing you could have done. If it were not for Oliver, you would have also perished.'

'Oliver? Your Mr Weir?'

'Yes, Henry, I will explain everything but we must go; they are coming for us.'

The stone slab above us began to shift and moonlight began to penetrate the darkness. Oliver stood over us. He held out his hand to me, and I reached out for it. My legs gave way as I tried to stand.

'What's the matter with her?' Henry asked.

'She refused to leave your side, refused to drink, and now you have taken her blood.' Oliver reprimanded. 'Please, Rose, let me carry you, or take some of my blood. You are too weak. They are near – you sense them too; I can feel you do.'

'If anyone is to carry her, it will be me. Step aside, Oliver, and let me rise.'

Oliver did as he was asked. He knew now was not the time to argue.

Henry stepped out from the grave and lifted me into his arms.

I looked to Oliver and he held out his wrist to me. I sunk my teeth in and drank of him. I could feel the surge of his lifeblood running throughout my body.